DOMINGO'S TRAIL

Vicious Mexican bandit, Estrada, is holding an American to ransom in the Sabinas Valley; he has arranged for two different expeditions to come and shower him with gold in return for a safe release. But a mysterious Mexican named Domingo appears, warning that the captive is dead and that Estrada means to slaughter them all. With the combined ransom parties now joined in their mission, they are ready for bloody battle. Can Domingo's advice be trusted? And will all who follow his perilous trail survive?

GREG MITCHELL

DOMINGO'S TRAIL

Complete and Unabridged

LINFORD
Leicester

First published in Great Britain in 2012 by
Robert Hale Limited
London

First Linford Edition
published 2014
by arrangement with
Robert Hale Limited
London

A catalogue record for this book is available
from the British Library.

ISBN 978–1–4448–1960–1

Published by
F. A. Thorpe (Publishing)
Anstey, Leicestershire

Set by Words & Graphics Ltd.
Anstey, Leicestershire
Printed and bound in Great Britain by
T. J. International Ltd., Padstow, Cornwall

This book is printed on acid-free paper

1

The large, elderly man across the hotel room finally stopped asking questions. Outside it was hot and the sound of hoofs and rumbling wheels came through the dusty window glass but Forbes Crossen was not there to take in the sights and sounds of San Antonio. He lowered his bushy eyebrows and fixed a pensive gaze on the lean, sun-darkened man sitting opposite. He hardly looked old enough to have the experience required and had neither the beard nor the fringed buckskins favoured by many other government scouts. If anything, he looked more like a cowhand, but reliable sources had advised that Bill Locker was the genuine article. Crossen's people had already made extensive inquiries before sounding him out.

'You have all the qualifications for the job, Mr Locker,' Crossen said as though announcing some hitherto unknown discovery. 'You speak Spanish, are a former army scout and have some knowledge of northern Mexico. But if you take on this task, you will also need to be the very soul of discretion. At least one man's life depends upon it.'

'Are you hinting that there might also be others?' Locker liked to know what was happening and strongly disliked unnecessary secrecy.

'Who knows?' The blank expression on Crossen's face was enough to signal that he had made the only comments he was prepared to make on that particular topic.

The scout was not one to beat about the bush. 'I can keep my mouth shut but you haven't really told me what I'm supposed to do. I don't even know how you found out about me or just who you are. If this is life-and-death business, I want to know what I'm getting into.'

Fearing that Locker was on the verge of walking out, the big man chose his words carefully. 'I have been advised that you are familiar with the Sabinas

River country and I need you to guide a man down into Mexico — a man with a large sum of money.'

'I suppose you realize that the country where you want me to go is crawling with bandits who would kill for a nickel. Does the man with the money know where he's being sent?'

'He knows. He volunteered for the task.'

'This sounds like a government job or maybe something illegal. I won't be involved in any deal that's likely to land me in trouble with the law.'

Crossen gave a grimace that was his version of a reassuring smile. 'You have nothing to fear there. The US government will give all the assistance it can, although this must appear to be a private matter. If help is needed, it will be given but not on any official basis. You are not being employed directly by the government.'

Locker still had a few doubts and looked at the other man suspiciously. 'It seems to me that the two hundred dollars a month you are offering is not going to be for an easy job. That's much more than I made as an army scout.'

'That's right. The task could be a dangerous one but you will be working with a very good man. Considerable resources have been made available to ensure the safe completion of this mission and those involved are entitled to some compensation for the risks involved. Will you take the job?'

Locker thought for a couple of seconds. He did not like mysterious ventures but a degree of curiosity finally overcame his caution and he said, 'I may as well give it a try, seeing as I am out of work at present. What happens now?'

Crossen explained. 'You are to equip yourself for a couple of weeks' horse-back travel. Horses will be provided but you must supply your own guns and ammunition. I'm authorized to pay you an amount for the purchase of any equipment you need. Do you have modern cartridge firearms?'

'Yes, I have a pair of converted Colt

.44s and a Spencer .56/50 carbine.'

'You haven't progressed to a Winchester or Henry repeater?'

Locker shook his head. 'The Spencer is not quite as modern but the .44 rimfire cartridges those other rifles use are not powerful enough. The Spencer has a bit more range and hits a hell of a lot harder. If I have to shoot someone I want to make sure that he's in no state to fire back. Are you expecting there will be shooting?'

'I hope there won't be, but travelling with large sums of money can be risky.'

Secretly pleased with his new recruit, Crossen reached into the side pocket of his black frock coat and produced a roll of notes together with a receipt book. He peeled off five twenty-dollar notes and passed them to Locker. Then he completed the details in the receipt book and said, 'Sign here. This will be enough for whatever you need and the stage fare to Eagle Pass. I will telegraph ahead when you confirm that you are booked on tomorrow night's coach.

Your new boss, Ike Lindsay, will meet you at the stage depot. Any questions?'

'Yes, when do I find out exactly what I am needed to do? The Sabinas Valley is not hard to find and plenty of folks on the border speak Spanish. What special skills do I have that a heap of others don't?'

'Last year you guided a military detachment into Mexico chasing Apaches. It was a politically risky situation and the army officers concerned were most impressed by your ability. It is on the recommendation of the military that I am hiring you. As to the current task, Lindsay will give you the details. At this stage it is safest that you don't know. But I can tell you this: the work is legal and highly important. For the safety of all concerned, it is best that you don't know the identity of your employers at this time.' With that announcement Crossen rose and extended a hand across the desk. 'Good luck. Just let me know when you have confirmed a place on the coach.'

Eagle Pass was a small town on a bluff above the Rio Grande, a mixture of sun-bleached timber buildings and flat-roofed adobe structures. It differed little from several similar-sized places in Texas except that it looked across the wide, brown river to the Mexican town of Piedras Negras on the river flats opposite. Neither town could be classed as a thriving metropolis. They were bases for cattlemen and a few small businesses but also sheltered the thieves and outlaws who raided on both sides of the border.

Locker found Ike Lindsay waiting for him when he alighted from the coach. He was a tall, powerfully built man, somewhere in his thirties, with the erect bearing of a soldier. Too big for the cavalry, Locker reckoned him to have been in the infantry or artillery. His face looked strangely youthful despite the odd grey streak in his black hair and short, neatly trimmed beard. The butt of a Smith & Wesson .44 protruded forward from under his coat on the left side. His handshake was firm and his smile friendly although he was sparing with words as though he feared eavesdroppers.

Another man stood near Lindsay. He was slightly older and of average size and build with bushy brown eyebrows and a large drooping moustache that made him appear like a human version of an Airedale Terrier. He too wore a six-gun on a belt with long rifle cartridges in the loops and his eyes moved constantly as though checking all around him. A careful man, Locker thought, with an air of dependability about him. Herman Frolech would be the third member of the team.

'Let's get you settled into the hotel, such as it is,' Lindsay said briskly. 'Then we can stroll across to the cantina for a meal. The food's just as good and it's best if we are not seen around the hotel too much. There are people there that I prefer to avoid and the less they see of our movements, the better.'

'This all sounds very mysterious. How much will I be told about what's going on?' asked Locker.

Lindsay replied, 'I'll tell you a lot more when we get clear of town but at present staying silent reduces the risk. Even Herman doesn't know the full story and he's been with me for years. It's safer if I am the only one who knows. If anything happens to me, you and Herman can abort the mission and you will still be paid.'

Herman spoke for the first time. 'That's assuming we can find this Crossen character again.'

'Don't worry,' Lindsay laughed. 'I will give both of you his business card when we are clear of Eagle Pass, just in case. But I don't intend getting killed for some time yet.'

* * *

Phillip Avery glared impatiently around the dining room of the badly misnamed

Palace Hotel, his broad features set in a scowl. He set great store in punctuality. Where was that woman? Time was important and the sooner he could finish this job and get back to regular detective work in some city, the better he would like it. He disliked western towns but had an uneasy feeling that Eagle Pass would be good compared to where they were going. The last five years of his thirty-year life had been spent working for the Pinkerton Detective Agency and he had established a reputation for reliability, but now that reputation seemed to be working against him. The agency had selected him as a bodyguard for a wealthy client responding to a Mexican bandit's ransom demand. By Avery's reasoning it was not a good idea but he was loyal to the agency.

Jenny Dixon had brought the five thousand dollars needed to free her mining engineer father but had insisted upon accompanying Avery when he paid over the money. The notion, to his

10

mind, was crazy and fraught with danger but the client had the money so the agency, with many misgivings, had agreed to her demands.

She entered the dining room at last and caught the attention of every man in the room. Not tall but with curly, dark hair, a pretty blue-eyed face and a neat figure, Miss Dixon would be noticed anywhere let alone a drab place like Eagle Pass. Her face broke into a dazzling smile as she recognized Avery and she turned every head in the room when she walked gracefully across to where the Pinkerton man waited.

He rose and pulled out a chair for her to be seated then returned to his side of the table.

'I hope I haven't kept you waiting, Mr Avery. I was sorting out what I would wear on our trip to Mexico.'

Avery looked worried. 'I wish you'd change your mind, Miss Dixon,' he said. 'Where we're going is very dangerous. Our guide has warned that we could be robbed before we even meet the men who are holding your father. The whole area is in turmoil and has been for years.'

'So you found a suitable guide?'

'I found a man who I hope will prove suitable, although I must admit that I have a few doubts about his character. His name is Sam Drysdale. He was part of General Shelby's command who refused to surrender after the civil war. They went into Mexico in sixty-five by the very route we will be taking. Later he came back the same way and he says that the country is still the same except that the Lipan Apaches are no longer a problem. The US and Mexican armies have hit them hard on both sides of the Rio Grande and some of our troops have even followed them into Mexican territory and taught them the error of their ways.'

'Surely that must have made things much safer,' Jenny suggested. Until that moment she had never heard of Lipan Apaches but saw no point in displaying her ignorance.

The detective frowned before replying. 'There are still bandits, revolutionaries and rogue soldiers down there. It would be much safer if you waited for us here.'

The dark curls bounced as the girl shook her head. 'I'm not afraid, Mr Avery. I have my own revolver and I can shoot. I have fired a whole box of cartridges through it so I know I could hit a man at close range if I had to. Don't forget too, that I am the only one who can identify my father. Suppose someone impersonated him just to get the money or even to escape from these people. I know that the ransom letter was in my father's handwriting but it is six months old.'

'That's what I mean,' Avery argued. 'There's too much uncertainty about this whole deal. The last thing we need is to get into a gunfight and you will find that shooting at a man is much harder than target shooting.'

She smiled sweetly. 'Mr Avery, the Pinkerton Agency raised no serious objections and they assure me that you are one of their best operatives. I'm sure you will be equal to the task.'

'I hope your confidence in me is not misplaced, because we are dealing with dangerous, scarcely civilized people. The instructions they mailed to us say we must be at a ruined village in the Sabinas Valley before the end of the month, but given the poor and very secret communications, there is much that can go wrong. To be frank, I have many doubts about this whole arrangement and would feel easier if you waited here in Eagle Pass. Our head office might have approved your coming with me but I feel that they are ignorant of the true situation.'

'It's no use arguing with me, Mr Avery. I'm going.'

The detective shrugged his broad shoulders and gave a rueful smile. 'So be it. I hope that you never have reason to regret your decision.'

'When do we leave?'

'Tomorrow night after dark. The Mexicans have some sort of Customs post at the border but it is not manned all night. By repute they are not to be trusted by anyone carrying large sums of money. We don't want them seizing it at the border so we'll creep across when the post is closed for the night.'

'And when do I meet our Mr Drysdale?'

'We'll see him in the morning but don't be too impatient because I doubt that you'll be impressed. Unfortunately, though, he is the only man we could get who has the right qualifications.'

2

Locker was used to rising early and before breakfast was ready at the hotel. He went directly to the corrals where Lindsay told him their horses were being kept. They were animals that the latter had personally selected; three for riding and one for a pack. Frolech joined him there and together they propped their elbows on the top rail and looked over the horses. All looked good serviceable types and had recently been shod.

'Have you and Lindsay selected your horses yet?' Locker asked.

'Lindsay has picked that dark brown horse in the corner but according to him, they're all much the same. He's a good judge of horses but I ain't fussy. Pick whatever one suits you and I'll take the other. The black horse is intended as a pack so you can pick between the bay horse with the white blaze or the roan.'

'I'll take the bay,' Locker said. 'They say colour doesn't matter but I am rather partial to a horse with a blaze and a white near-hind foot. It has probably been only a coincidence but I've seen a few very good horses that were marked like that.'

'Suit yourself. That big roan will do me.' Frolech glanced at the sun. 'I reckon it's time for breakfast. Lindsay will probably be there by now.'

Frolech's prediction was wrong. The only other diners were a beautiful dark-haired girl and a powerfully built man seated on the opposite side of the room. They were deep in conversation and paid little attention to the new arrivals.

Locker was curious. 'Who are they? He's not old enough to be her father but he don't look like he's married to her.'

'He's been hangin' around town for a couple of days. The lady arrived the night before last. That big feller minds his own business and we mind ours but Lindsay keeps out of his way.'

'Is he scared of him?'

Frolech snorted and leaned closer to the scout as though imparting some great secret. 'Listen to me, sonny. Ike Lindsay ain't scared of any man but he's smart enough to avoid unnecessary trouble. If Ike is keepin' away from someone, he has a damn good reason.'

Breakfast arrived and the couple were forgotten as both men settled down to some serious eating. Locker looked up halfway through his meal in time to see the others leaving. A short while later, Lindsay joined them.

'Looks like someone slept in,' Frolech growled.

His boss laughed. 'Wrong again, Herman. I could have been here earlier but I was waiting for that couple to leave.'

Frolech fixed him with an accusing gaze. 'I suppose you can't tell us why in case we blab it all over Texas.'

'I can tell you. That man is a Pinkerton operative named Avery. I have seen him in Washington and I would prefer that he doesn't see too much of me at present. His presence here could mean trouble for us.'

'Do you reckon he could be trackin' us?' Frolech suddenly seemed concerned.

'Could be. Pinkertons will work for anyone if the money is right and the job is not too illegal. Some jobs they take on are a bit doubtful so it's best we steer clear of them. I am worried, though, because if Avery is interested in us, someone has been talking. We're heading out today but I don't want anyone to know that we're aiming for Mexico. We will go north along the river until it's dark. Then we sneak back here and cross into Mexico.'

'Why come back?' Locker asked. 'I know a crossing a few miles upriver. We slipped a cavalry patrol across there last year while chasing Apaches. Our commander didn't want to worry the

Mexicans about us being there. Sometimes they agreed to these pursuits but other times they didn't, so it was less complicated if the Mexicans didn't know.'

Lindsay looked doubtful. 'Can you pick up the Sabinas River from there?'

'Sure can. Once away from the river flats we can head straight west over the first range of mountains and the Sabinas is on the other side.'

'Is anyone else likely to be at this crossing?'

'No reason for them to be. It's in rough, barren country where nobody needs to go.'

'That's good. You and Herman get packed up. I'll see you at the corral as soon as I settle our hotel bill.'

* * *

Sam Drysdale was in a foul mood. His daily hangover did that to him. If there had been a mirror on the wall of the stable where he had been sleeping, he would have seen a bearded, dirty face with a blood-shot eye on each side of a nose flattened in some long-forgotten brawl. His tousled black hair was streaked with grey and there was a slight stoop to his massive frame that made him look older than his forty years. His hips were aching as a reminder that he had fallen asleep still wearing his gun-belt with its big Smith & Wesson .44 on one side and a massive Bowie knife on the other. He looked around in the hay, found his worn buckskin jacket and pulled it on over his faded red undershirt. Then, jamming a crumpled, black hat on his head, he was ready to face the day. He had a job again and had celebrated that fact a little too enthusiastically the night before. He disliked the idea of returning to Mexico but years had passed and things were slightly more orderly than the last time he had been there. The current situation would be different because he was reasonably confident that none remembered his last sojourn

21

beyond the Rio Grande. Most likely he had been forgotten in the upheaval as the Mexicans battled the French and Austrians. Now, with the foreigners driven out, they were fighting among themselves. Even as he steeled himself to walk out into the glaring sunlight, he mentally crossed his fingers and hoped that all would be well. The idea of breakfast did not appeal to him so he headed straight for the corrals where Avery, his new boss, said he would meet him.

Locker and Frolech were busy packing supplies and saddling horses. The scout had already saddled his bay and hung a leather case with field glasses on one side of the saddle horn and a Blakeslee cartridge box containing ten quick-loading, seven-shot tubes of Spencer ammunition on the other side.

Frolech hung a long, .50 Springfield breech-loader by its sling from his saddle horn, intending to sling it over his back when mounted.

'You don't like repeaters, Herman?'

'Not yet I don't. They ain't got enough range. When they make 'em stronger I might be interested. Lindsay likes 'em — you can see one of them new Winchesters there on his saddle — but I don't reckon they're as good as I want a rifle to be. Since the war I haven't had a lot of use for a rifle and hope that situation continues. The less I have to fire one, the better I'll like it, so I reckon this one will do me.'

Drysdale frowned as he saw the two men working in the corral. It was closest to the shed where he and Avery had stored their supplies and in his present mood he did not fancy carrying saddles or packs any further than was needed.

He strode up to Locker and, in a voice laden with new-found authority, demanded, 'How much longer will you fellers be usin' this here corral?'

'Can't say for sure,' Locker replied. 'Depends when our boss gets here.'

'You've gotta move. I need this

corral. I'm on urgent business — Pinkerton Agency business.'

'We won't be here much longer,' Locker said mildly. 'I'm sure Pinkertons can wait a while.'

Drysdale had not expected that reply because he thought that his temporary employment had given him some sort of legal status. He paused for a couple of seconds, considered his options and then chose the wrong one. He brushed his jacket back from the butt of his gun, put his face close to Locker's and snarled, 'I'm givin' the orders around here. You and your mangy sidekick better get yourselves, your horses and your fixin's out of this corral right now while you can still walk.'

Locker's reply came in the form of a vicious left rip into the bigger man's short ribs. Almost paralyzed with pain, the recipient bent forward in an effort to catch his breath and leaned into a smashing right hand that knocked him flat on his back. No sooner had he hit the ground than Locker had snatched away his gun and knife.

'Get up very slow,' he ordered. 'It would be a shame to have to kill you just for being impatient, ugly and just plain stupid.'

Frolech picked up his rifle and said casually, 'Those are pretty good reasons by my book.'

Drysdale rolled onto one elbow, shook his head to clear it and, as his breath returned, mumbled some obscenity under his breath. Struggling to his feet he fixed his assailant with a malevolent stare before stating, 'You can't attack a Pinkerton man and get away with it.'

'I can if they're all as useless as you. Now, get the hell out of here. I'll leave your weapons at the corral. If I see you coming back with any sort of a gun I'll kill you.'

'And if he don't, I will,' Frolech growled, displaying the long rifle he was holding, ready to fire.

'You caught me by surprise,' Drysdale muttered angrily. 'Next time we meet I'll come shootin'.'

'I'll remember that,' Locker promised. He watched until his late opponent had walked away and before he resumed his packing, asked Frolech, 'Do you know that fella?'

'I've seen him around and mostly he's been drunk but it sounds like he's workin' for that Pinkerton detective.'

'They can't be too fussy who they hire.'

'At times they ain't. In the cities they'll recruit the worst kind of skullbusters to settle disputes with underpaid workers who sometimes dare to object to bein' short-changed on their wages. Pinkertons will uphold any law that might bring a buck or two their way.'

Lindsay arrived shortly after, and frowned when he was told what had happened. 'I was hoping that nobody would take much notice of us. We'll need to get out of here fairly quickly. If Pinkertons are sniffing around they might be looking at us.'

'Why should they?' Locker asked suspiciously. 'If there is something wrong about this deal I want to know about it.'

'I assure you there's nothing illegal,' Lindsay replied. 'However it is politically sensitive government business. I'll explain more when we're on the trail.'

Locker was more curious than ever. 'But if this is government business why would Pinkertons be spying on us?'

Lindsay said quietly after looking around as though he feared being overheard, 'Pinkertons are a private organization who will work for whoever pays their fees. If they are on our trail it means that someone highly placed in government has either been careless or downright treacherous. Our mission is supposed to be secret.'

'It don't look all that secret now,' Frolech growled as he slung his rifle over his shoulder.

3

Two hours' ride north of Eagle Pass, Locker halted his horse on a bluff overlooking the wide, brown Rio Grande. From that height no ford was visible but a couple of distinctive, water-worn rocks were showing and he knew they were at a place where he had crossed before.

'You can't see it, but there's a safe crossing there,' he told the others. 'Indian raiders and bandits have used it regularly. We used it about a year ago when I guided a cavalry detachment across here.'

Lindsay halted his horse beside Locker's bay. 'Did you go anywhere near the valley of the Sabinas River?'

The scout pointed to the west. 'We sure did. It's just behind that line of mountains over there.'

'Do you know of an abandoned

village up near the headwaters of the river?'

'I do. That's a place never forgotten by anyone who has seen it. Back in sixty-five, the Lipan Apaches wiped out the whole village. Not long after, General Shelby and the rest of his no-surrender men had a big fight to cross the river further upstream. The Confederates won but the crossing cost them a few casualties. By all accounts, though, Shelby's men killed a heap of Indians. Since then the Lipans have scattered into small bands that are harder for soldiers to find, but a few are still around. Why are we going to that village?'

'We have to meet some Mexicans there and ransom an American mining engineer. He was captured by bandits and sent a message to us saying it will take five thousand dollars to get him released.'

'So we will be trotting around bandit-infested country with all that cash?'

Lindsay nodded. 'That's right, and

that's why it is so important that nobody discovers we have that much money. It will be safer still if nobody even sees us. Three men is a small enough party to hide but hardly big enough to defend itself. A larger group might be safer but would be noticed and it could make the Mexican government a bit too curious.'

'That makes sense but why do we need to be afraid of Pinkertons?'

'The engineer, Dixon, was on a special job paid for by a supposedly private group of mining interests with strong political connections. If they misuse Dixon's findings, a lot of bad things could happen and the government might not survive the political uproar that is likely to follow. Dixon never reported back and our job is to get him and his report into government hands. Right now I'm starting to think that someone on the other side of Congress has somehow got wind of this little expedition and has set Pinkertons on our trail.'

'I'll make our trail a tough one to follow but Pinkertons are the least of our worries once we get over the river. We won't find too many friends among bandits and wandering groups of Lipan Apaches who might pick up our tracks.'

'Let's hope we're not discovered,' Lindsay said. 'Now get us over the river.'

*   *   *

Jenny was glad that Avery had warned her about Drysdale otherwise she would not have considered making a hazardous journey in his company. Nothing about his appearance inspired confidence and he was bad-mannered and uncommunicative, as though nursing a grudge against the world. Her fears were slightly allayed when she found that the guide obviously knew the country well and even in the dead of night, was picking up the necessary landmarks.

A fourth member had joined their party, a poorly dressed young man with the dark features of an Indian. He called himself Tomás and when inclined, he could speak both English and Spanish but mostly he remained silent and only spoke when directly addressed. A large sheath knife dangled from one side of his belt and a Henry rifle was slung across his back. He had offered his services when he saw that Avery was packing for some sort of journey. The detective was reluctant to take on another helper but Drysdale said that he would be useful for looking after the packhorse and the spare animal they had brought to bring home the ransomed man. 'This *hombre* won't cost you much and he can look after the stock so I can do some proper scoutin',' he explained. He felt it was not necessary to tell the others that the new recruit would also relieve him of practically all camp chores.

Avery agreed with the idea and, mainly to make conversation, he asked Drysdale about their destination, the abandoned village on the upper Sabinas River.

'It was a nice little place when we stopped there with Shelby. Later I heard that the Lipans massacred every livin' soul and left bodies everywhere. The Mexicans reckon it's haunted and I've heard that nobody goes there now.'

'Were you part of Shelby's command?'

'In a way. I was never in the army but a few of us Texans decided to join him rather than live under Yankee rule. I knew the country and helped guide the force but I never settled in Mexico like some of them did because I found the Mexican government to be worse than the Yankees. Shelby was a bit slower to catch on and stayed there for a couple of years, but I think the whole caboodle returned to US eventually.'

Jenny stayed quiet and merely followed the others. She could see little of the country around her and was not used to riding at night. Sometimes she heard the distant barking of a dog and thought she glimpsed man-made structures through the gloom, but eventually these sights and sounds became fewer. About an hour after they had skirted the Mexican town she was sure that the party had moved into an area that was sparsely inhabited — if anyone lived there at all.

The country changed gradually and as the ground rose it became harder and stonier. Their progress was marked by sparks that the horseshoes had struck from the flinty rocks along the invisible trail that they seemed to be following.

Tomás was taking his new job seriously and once after they had climbed a steep rise, he called softly to suggest that they should rest their horses for a while.

Drysdale agreed and the party halted on a ridge. The guide pointed north-west to where a long, dark wall could be seen on the horizon. 'See that gap in the mountains over there? That's the Sabinas Valley.'

'How far is it?' Jenny asked.

'It's another day and a bit of ridin'.'

34

Just before dawn we can camp at a little spring I used to know where we can rest safely.' He turned to Tomás and said, 'You've been there more recent than me. Do you know a little box canyon with grass and water a few miles ahead?'

The young man touched a match to a cigarette rolled in corn husk and puffed on it a couple of times before finally replying, '*Sí*, I know where you mean. It will be a good place to camp.'

'How safe is it?' Avery asked.

Drysdale replied, 'Both the Mexican and American armies have broken up the big Apache bands so them that's left are scattered. There could be a few bandits about but I reckon them that are holding the young lady's father will make sure that we ain't troubled by minor crooks. They don't want anyone else gettin' away with their *dinero*. There's still things that could go wrong but our chances of gettin' in and out are pretty good.'

Jenny expressed her greatest doubt.

'What's to stop these kidnappers just killing us and taking the money?'

Avery told her, 'Nothing except that maybe they don't want to lose a few men. I'll try to negotiate a peaceful exchange but can give no guarantees. I want you to keep well in the background in that Mexican serape and sombrero I bought you and hope that no one notices, because if they realize that you are a woman, they might also decide to hold you for ransom. Nobody in head office seemed inclined to listen when I said that your very presence greatly increased our danger, so now you will have first-hand experience if things go wrong. If possible I will try to carry out negotiations away from our horses, where I want you to wait.'

'But you need me,' Jenny reminded him. 'I am the only one who can identify my father.'

'You can do that from a distance. I have a small but powerful telescope and you can make the identification from a safe distance with that.'

'That's provided we see 'em comin',' Drysdale growled. 'Some of these *bandidos* have done a lot of fighting with Apaches and are damn near as good at skulkin' about.'

'Do you reckon they will deal with us honestly?' Jenny asked.

'I ain't sure they've had much practice at doin' anything the honest way. Some of them are real sons-abitches.'

'Watch your language, there's a lady present,' snapped Avery.

Drysdale glared at him. 'What are you gonna do if I don't? I tell things as they are and if you don't like it, you can fire me. Then see how far you get.'

Jenny said quickly, 'I'm sure Mr Drysdale was not being deliberately offensive and we can't let an argument over manners jeopardize this expedition. Thank you Mr Avery for your concern but I can look after myself. It is vital that we stick to the main purpose and forget minor lapses.'

Avery shrugged his shoulders. 'Miss

Dixon, as you are the one paying the bills I'm happy to do some things your way but remember, when we meet up with those bandits, what I say goes.'

'Now,' Jenny said pleasantly, 'let's find that camp you were talking about. I'm not used to long hours in the saddle.'

Tomás held her horse as she mounted. They were some distance from the others and he said softly as he looked in Drysdale's direction, 'Stay away from that man. He is danger.'

'What do you mean?'

But Tomás had already walked back to his own scrawny paint horse as though he had said all he intended saying on that subject.

They started off again into the blackness, relieved only by the star-studded sky. Jenny hoped that Drysdale knew where he was going; the terse warning from Tomás had just added to her doubts.

4

Locker had them on the trail early next day. It had been a dry camp with no fire and sleeping on the hard, uneven ground was not comfortable, even for those who had done it for years.

'How far are we from the abandoned village?' Lindsay asked as he surveyed the scene from the mountain top. Below was a barren landscape, a winding valley of black lava rocks, cactus and mesquite. The course of the Sabinas River was marked with a few ancient Spanish oaks and cotton-woods and in places seemed to disappear. Only glimpses of sparkling water seen through the foliage and the odd patch of green grass along the banks hinted that the valley had a few more useful areas.

'I wouldn't like to be tryin' to make a livin' offa that country,' Frolech growled, 'not unless there was a market

39

for rattlesnakes and Gila monsters.'

Locker pointed to a bend in the valley. 'The village is around that bend but it's best if we stay high until we get opposite it. If anyone is planning a nasty surprise, they'll be watching along the river. There's an old trail that runs beside it. We can keep off the skyline and make our way quietly along the high ground where we have a good chance of seeing what goes on down in the valley.'

'There's smoke over there.' Frolech pointed to the east where a thin column of white smoke rose against the clear blue sky. 'Do you reckon it's Apaches?'

'No. Indians are smarter than that. It's not a signal, just a camp fire of some sort. It's as good a way as I know to attract trouble.'

Lindsay looked down the valley and said, 'The smoke has stopped. Whoever it is, they've put out the fire.'

'Sounds like someone had an attack of brains,' Frolech muttered.

'I hope they weren't too late,' Locker

told him. 'The Apaches are early risers and they look all around as soon as it's light. The odds are that they saw that smoke. You can bet they'll have a look around just in case it came from a soldier camp.'

'How big a threat are the Apaches?' Lindsay asked.

The scout replied, 'We won't have to fight hundreds of them like Shelby had to do when he came up the Sabinas. The bands are scattered now into small bunches but even three or four Apaches can cause us a lot of grief. With plenty of care and a bit of luck, though, a small group like us has a good chance of getting in and out of here without attracting too much attention. I think those kidnappers could be our biggest threat.'

'Maybe it was them had the fire,' Frolech suggested.

'I would have expected them to be further up the valley near the old village,' Locker said, 'but bad characters survive longest when they don't do what people expect.'

They started off again keeping just below the skyline and staying under cover of trees and large boulders where possible for another two hours. The presence of someone else in the vicinity had given the trio the incentive to remain unobserved. Although the others were miles out of earshot, nobody spoke or made unnecessary noise.

At one rocky spur where pines and brush offered concealment, they halted. Both Locker and Lindsay had field glasses and carefully studied the river valley below. The latter looked ahead and after searching the landscape for a while, announced, 'I can see the village. I can just make out what looks like a couple of adobe walls.'

'That's where it should be,' Locker told him, but made no attempt to look upriver. He fiddled with the glasses for a while and said quietly, 'I think I can see our *bandidos*. There's a bunch of riders coming up the valley. They look like white men and Mexicans.'

'How many?'

'Looks like four with a couple of spare horses. But they're coming from the opposite direction than what I thought.'

Lindsay turned and trained his glasses down the valley. 'I can see two Anglos in front. The third one looks like a little Mex, all sombrero and serape, and the last one with the loose horses could be anything — might be a half-breed. It's hard to tell.'

'I can't see anyone looks like he might be a prisoner,' Locker said.

Lindsay sounded worried as he replied, 'Me neither. Could this be some sort of doublecross?'

'I don't know. They might just be travellers. Wait, I can see a dust cloud back about a mile behind them. That could be the rest of the bunch. These might be scouting ahead. What do you want to do?'

'It's a day too early for the ransom meeting. Let's keep undercover and move on to the ruined village. Do you know of a place where we can lie low and just see what these people are up to?'

'There's a big stand of trees just over the river from the village. We can hide there until we find out what the hell is happening.'

On the trail beside the river, Avery urged his mount up level with Drysdale's. The latter was looking around as he rode, as though suspicious of something, while he chewed slowly on the wad of tobacco in his cheek.

'How close are we to the village?'

The guide spat before answering. 'It should be around the next bend, but from what I've been told, there mightn't be much of it left. It's a pity. It was a good little place when I came through with Shelby. Them murderin' Apaches killed everyone after that.'

Riding a couple of horse lengths behind, Jenny heard the sounds but took a while to identify the cause. Then she realized that it was the pounding of horses' feet, growing louder every second.

Thoroughly alarmed, she turned to Tomás who was riding behind, apparently half asleep. 'Tomás,' she called. 'I can hear horses coming up behind us.'

The young half-breed grunted something the girl did not understand, checked his horse and looked back.

By this time Avery and Drysdale had also heard the approaching hoofbeats. The former twisted in his saddle but could not see far behind because of a bend in the narrow valley. 'Someone's coming up behind us. You'd better come up here with me, Miss Dixon,' he shouted.

Jenny urged her mount into a trot and as she neared the other two, she saw that Drysdale had turned pale and his eyes were darting about like a man about to be confronted by his greatest dread.

Their guide's fears were well justified when, two hundred yards behind them, a party of wild riders galloped into view from behind the bend in the trail. War cries burst from several throats when they saw their quarry ahead.

'It's Lipan Apaches — we can't fight 'em in the open,' Drysdale shouted. The terror in his voice was obvious. 'Head for the village.' After that command, he spurred his horse away from the others.

Avery hesitated long enough for Jenny to join him and then they too plunged into the dust cloud that the scout's horse was kicking up. The instinct for survival had taken over and fear was pushed into the background as they urged their mounts to top speed.

The Apaches tried a couple of long-range shots that missed by wide margins but their swift, sure-footed ponies were gaining on the pursued at every stride.

Jenny dared not take her eyes off the rocky ground ahead and prayed that her pony would not stumble or fall as it galloped, neck stretched and head low, among the scattered rocks and uneven patches of trail. Avery's faster horse pulled away; the detective had forgotten his companion. They swept around the shoulder of a rocky spur and there ahead they saw trees, tall weeds and a few adobe walls on a clear patch of gently sloping hillside.

Avery's mount, despite its greater burden, was quicky drawing away from Jenny. A horse was suddenly racing beside hers. She was looking ahead thinking that it might have been the spare animal or Tomás's mount crowding her on a narrow stretch of trail bordering the river-bank. Cramped for room, her pony shortened its stride and threw up its head as it struggled to stay on its feet. Then in the dust and chaos, something hit her on the side of the head, knocking her from the saddle and landing her unconscious in a patch of sand on the river-bank, four feet below the trail. It was only luck that she landed close to the steep bank and remained unobserved as the Apache riders pounded along the trail a few feet above her.

Avery and Drysdale reached the

shelter of the first ruin, jumped from their saddles and, rifles in hand, sought shelter behind a partially collapsed adobe wall. It afforded some degree of cover and from there they started firing on the Apaches at rapidly decreasing range. A stricken horse reared over backwards, collapsing in the dust cloud it had helped create. One rider came right up to the wall before Avery planted a bullet in his chest and knocked him from his mount. Another warrior burst through the swirling dust and gunsmoke turning his mount side-on so that he could fire a shotgun full of slugs one-handed across the wall. Drysdale beat him to the shot by a fraction of a second and a .50 calibre bullet from his stubby Ball carbine ended the attacker's career.

For a couple of seconds all was confusion beyond the wall. Both white men had repeaters and fired them as rapidly as they could. Hampered by loose horses and fallen riders with their targets partly obscured by dust and powder smoke, the Apaches quickly reached the conclusion that a frontal assault would be too costly. They halted only long enough to gather up their fallen comrades and then galloped back behind the bend in the trail.

A feeling of relief swept over Avery as he saw the Indians retreat. He was frantically dropping bullets into his Henry repeater's magazine tube when he suddenly realized that Jenny and Tomás were missing. Turning to face Drysdale he demanded, 'Where's Jenny Dixon?'

At first the scout seemed too shocked to answer. His hands were shaking and there were a few seconds' delay before he finally croaked, 'I don't know. I thought she was just behind us.' Then he added, 'Forget about her. She's dead and probably the greaser too. We've gotta look after ourselves now.'

Avery swore savagely and then growled, 'Can this mess get any worse? Do you realize that we just lost the one person who could identify Dixon? And the ransom money's in my saddle-bag. Who knows where in the blue blazes my horse is now? Everything's going to hell in a hand basket.'

Drysdale's assessment was hardly comforting. 'Forget about all that. It can get a whole heap worse yet. We have to look after ourselves. Those are Lipan Apaches and they are some of the meanest critters that ever drew breath. If they capture us, bein' skinned alive is one of the more pleasant things that's likely to happen.'

5

From the shelter of the trees Locker had a good view of what was happening across the river. He drew his carbine, checked the sights and told the others, 'I think it's time we took a hand in this.'

'I don't,' Lindsay snapped. 'We don't know who those people are and if they stay in those ruins they could jeopardize the whole ransom deal. That's where we have to meet Dixon's kidnappers. They could even be part of the gang.'

'You mean you would let three people die to save one?'

'That one is mighty important to our government. I know it sounds hard but rushing in there might not be the best move in this situation.'

Locker had no such doubts. 'I can see that little Mexican lying under the river-bank. He's starting to stir. When the Apaches see him, he's gone for sure.

At present I rate those strangers down there as being in as much need as your kidnapped government *hombre*. You can do what you like but I'm taking a hand.'

'I'm in charge here, Locker. We wait.'

'I just resigned,' the scout announced. He urged his mount down the slope to the edge of the trees.

The Apaches had dismounted and were working their way forward, crouching low and using every bit of available cover. They intended no suicide charges into the muzzles of two repeating rifles. Stealth would serve their purposes much better.

Consciousness returned to Jenny. She could hear gunfire; some of it was very close. Then the memory of the Indians came back with a rush. She could not quite recall how she had reached the position she was in but knew she was in grave danger. Worse still, she could hear the Apaches calling to each other — they were not far away. Soft footfalls sounded on the bank just above her and she fancied she could hear someone breathing. She cowered back against the bank, aware that she had a revolver on her belt but fearful that any movement would alert the person standing just above her. Then the inevitable happened.

An Apache warrior, small, wiry and bow-legged, seeking better cover, jumped down off the bank and landed like a big cat beside her. His hideously painted face seemed to contort in surprise as he found himself standing beside an enemy. Instinctively Jenny kicked out and her riding boot connected solidly with the warrior's shin. He staggered slightly and swung his rifle muzzle to cover his attacker. As he cocked the hammer on his Sharps carbine, he muttered something unintelligible to his terrified victim.

Jenny tried to draw her gun but its hammer became entangled in the folds of her over-large serape. Seeing her predicament, the warrior smiled, his white teeth showing in contrast to his dark and painted face.

She flinched as she heard the shot but no bullet tore into her. The warrior

53

spun around, dropped his gun and fell backwards into the river. It was then that she saw powder smoke among the trees on the opposite bank. Someone was firing rapidly into the exposed flank of the attackers. She did not dare raise her head to see what damage the new arrival was doing but then more rifles joined in.

Caught in a crossfire, the Apaches made a hasty retreat. They paused to collect their casualties but apparently decided that the corpse in the river was too exposed to attempt to retrieve it. In seconds, all had disappeared from view with only the gunsmoke hanging in the air to indicate that the area had been a scene of such conflict.

'Hold your fire,' a voice called from the other bank. 'I'm coming across.'

A man with a rifle in his hand emerged from the trees and set his bay horse into the shallow, rocky stream. A few yards behind him, two more riders and a packhorse appeared.

Fearing that the Apaches might

return, Jenny rose to her feet and ran towards the ruined village where she could see Avery and Drysdale carefully peering over the crumbling walls.

Locker's horse had reached the other bank just as the girl drew level. From the height of his saddle, the scout could not see the small person beneath the big sombrero and laughingly said, 'Hey, *amigo*, you can slow down now. The Indians have gone for a while.'

Only when Jenny stopped did Locker realize that the legs protruding beneath the serape were not in trousers but a divided skirt. She looked up, showing a pale, very pretty, feminine face where the scout had expected to see the brown features and dark eyes of a Mexican boy. Now it was his turn to be surprised.

'You're a lady,' he gasped. 'I'm sorry, I thought you were a Mexican kid.'

Jenny had recovered her composure enough to smile. 'If it was you who shot that Indian back there, consider yourself forgiven. I really thought I was about to die.'

'That could still happen yet. You'd best get over there with your friends before those Apaches come back.'

As the girl hurried to the ruins, Locker remained watching for the attackers. He was sure they would be back once they assessed the odds against them. Lindsay and Frolech joined him on the river-bank but the former was not looking very happy.

'So you changed your mind?' Locker challenged.

'There wasn't much point in staying out when you took a hand but if this job goes wrong I'll hold you responsible.'

'Do what you like but I'm going to see who these strangers are and how they fit into things. I ain't in the least bit sorry about saving that girl's life. You can decide how to handle this problem later, Lindsay, but for the present we all need to stick together.'

'You're right there, Locker, and you're still on the payroll but don't make a habit of insubordination.'

Avery stayed close to cover as the three riders approached. His concern was obvious and he looked about him as though the newcomers were not his main priority.

Drysdale glowered when he saw who had rescued them and both Locker and Frolech smiled knowingly when they recognized him.

The Pinkerton man seemed distracted, paying little attention to his rescuers as though they were of little importance. 'I need my horse,' he said by way of greeting. 'It got away during the shooting. Could you get it for me? I think it ran off away from the Indians. It's very important.'

'Just hold on a minute,' Locker told him. 'Chances are that the Apaches have it already and right now things are more important than lost horses. I'm Bill Locker. The gent with the scowl is Lindsay and the other one's Frolech. I guess you're the Pinkerton man your whiskery friend over there was telling me about.'

Avery glared at Drysdale. He had not been told of the confrontation with Locker. 'Have you been talking to people?'

'I told him I was workin' for a Pinkerton man, that's all.'

'Even that was too much. Now make yourself useful and find my horse.'

Drysdale stared at Avery as though the latter had suddenly lost his senses. 'I ain't goin' from here. Those Apaches could be all around us.'

Lindsay interrupted. 'Unless I miss my guess, your name is Avery. I think I've seen you in Washington.'

'I thought I'd seen you too, but couldn't quite figure out where. This young lady is Miss . . . er, Smith . . . Jenny Smith. It seems you already know Drysdale.'

Locker said urgently, 'Let's forget the formalities. Those Apaches are probably regrouping. We need to get the horses behind some of these walls and then find a good spot to shoot from.' He turned to Jenny. 'Miss Smith, do you reckon you could hold the horses? We'll need every man with a rifle that we can get.'

The girl had recovered very quickly after her narrow escape and said in a surprsingly calm voice, 'I'll hold them, Mr Locker. Just show me the best place to be.'

'I have to get my horse,' Avery insisted. Then he said to Drysdale, 'If you want to get paid I want you to go and find my horse. You're supposed to be a scout. You should be able to track it.'

'You couldn't pay me enough money to go out there, Avery. If you want that horse so badly, go and get it yourself.'

'My horse is missing too,' Jenny said, 'and so is Tomás and our spare horse and packhorse.'

'Do you know what happened to Tomás?' Avery asked the girl.

'The Apaches must have got him. He was behind me when one of them knocked me off my horse. I suppose he's dead.'

'Serves him right,' Drysdale snarled. 'He could have been in cahoots with them. He was too careless, lightin' matches on hilltops at night, and leavin' the camp fire burnin' after daybreak. He probably attracted those murderin' skunks. Serves him right if they killed him.'

'You left it a bit late to warn him about being careless,' Avery accused. With every passing minute his confidence in his scout was diminishing rapidly.

'We was told that the armies on both sides of the border had scattered the Lipans and there was only little groups hidin' out in the mountains. I never thought they could get together enough fightin' men to cause trouble.'

'We heard the same story,' Locker said, 'but I reckon they had nearly twenty men. That's a lot for an Apache war party. Something big must have brought them together.'

Frolech had not joined in the discussion but remained alert, looking back downriver in the direction that the Indians had retreated. 'I can see something stirrin' in the brush down there. Best get undercover and talk later.'

6

This time there was no sudden onslaught. It was more carefully planned. Unseen snipers started to fire from the brush with firearms ranging from smooth-bore muskets and various carbines to at least one modern repeater. Screened by brush and an increasing haze of powder smoke, the shooters offered no definite targets to the defenders.

'No point in wasting lead,' Lindsay observed. 'Let's wait until they try to rush us. Getting across that open ground in front will cost them a lot of men.'

'They ain't that dumb,' Locker told him. He flinched momentarily as a musket ball skimmed a protective wall and sprayed him with adobe dust, then continued. 'They'll try to work around us while a couple of shooters keep us busy. There's too much open ground on the river side for that trick but there's a bit of cover for them on our right where the ground slopes up to the cliffs. I reckon that's where they'll go.'

'I agree.' Frolech said. 'There's about four hundred yards of room for them to move around us. We need someone further out on our right to stop them.'

'I ain't volunteerin',' Drysdale announced, making no effort to conceal the fear in his voice.

Frolech glared at him contemptuously. 'Nobody's askin' you. I'll go. My rifle can cover that area if I get in the right spot.'

'I'll go with you,' Locker said. 'You need a repeating rifle with you. If you take the long-range shots, I can keep the others from getting too close.'

Avery objected. 'I am not sure that we should be dividing our forces.'

Lindsay had no such doubts. 'We should still be close enough to support each other and it's a damn sight better than getting surrounded.'

Frolech picked up his rifle and nodded to Locker. 'We go, then. You pick the safest way and I'll follow.'

Avery still looked doubtful but Drysdale said nothing as he clutched his rifle and fearfully cowered behind the broken wall. Locker doubted that he would be much use in a fight but Lindsay and Avery seemed made of sterner stuff and both had repeating rifles. He made a slight detour to the roofless ruin where Jenny was holding the horses. Fortunately the walls were high enough to shelter the stock and they could only leave by one narrow door.

'Miss Smith,' he said, 'Herman and I are going up the hill a bit to stop the Apaches getting around us, so if you hear shooting it will not be Indians. If those horses start getting jumpy, try to pull one across the doorway so they won't see the opening and try to rush out. Be careful that you don't get knocked down, because you are likely to be trampled.'

The girl summoned up a smile. 'Thank you. Nobody else took the trouble to tell me what's going on. What's your name?'

'I'm Bill Locker but just Bill will suit me fine.'

'I'm Jenny Di — , er Smith.' She remembered just in time. 'You saved my life so don't be too formal. Just call me Jenny.'

Glancing around, the scout saw a couple of rails that had once been part of a corral. He carried them to the door of the ruin and, taking a rope from a nearby saddle, rigged them across the open door in an improvised gate. 'These poles are half rotted,' he told Jenny, 'but they should discourage any horse trying its luck with the open doorway if you find you can't hold them all. If they get too restless and you are worried, slip under the rails and take your chances outside. Herman and I will make sure that no Apaches get in a position to get a shot at you.'

'Thank you, Bill,' the girl said and managed another nervous smile. 'You keep the Indians away and I'll make sure that these horses stay where they're supposed to.'

With a nod to Frolech, Locker crouched low and crept out behind a screen of weeds and cactus. The older man allowed him to go about twenty yards before following. Progress was slow and in places Locker had to drop down and crawl, an exercise made even more painful by the hot sun and sharp rocks littering the stony ground. His objective was a small cluster of rocks roughly midway between the ruins and the cliffs. It had a commanding view back along the river and a rifleman there could prevent the Apaches slipping around behind their defences. He could see one problem as he came closer to the rocks; the last few yards would be across bare ground and he was sure that the Apaches would see them. Then there was another doubt that caused him even greater concern: what if the Lipans had the same idea and were already at the rocks? There was only one way to find out. He sprung erect and, with his rifle at the ready, sprinted for the rocks.

The Apaches saw him and fired a couple of shots in his direction but because of the element of surprise, the bullets did not come close. Frolech saw no point in advertising his presence and remained undercover until a few more shots were fired at Locker's refuge. He reasoned that many of the warriors would have single-shot weapons and waited for a lull in the firing that indicated they were re-loading. Then he made his run for the rocks. Something hissed past his ear and a heavy lead ball kicked up a fountain of dirt at his feet. He heard Locker firing rapidly, throwing lead into the brush where powder smoke betrayed the presence of a shooter. It was unlikely that he would score a hit but the shots would be close enough to disconcert the rifleman. Panting heavily but unscathed, Frolech threw himself into the welcome shelter of the boulders. 'I'm gettin' too old for this sort of stuff,' he grunted as he lowered himself behind a boulder.

The rocks afforded good cover and the Apaches wasted no ammunition. Peering through a narrow gap between two boulders Locker said, 'It's lucky we got here first, we can see a fair bit from here. It will cost the Apaches dearly if they try to get past this spot.'

'You know 'em better than me,' Frolech muttered as he studied the landscape. 'Do you think they might try to rush us?'

'Probably not. If they try to attack us here they will probably try creeping up on us so we'd best keep a sharp eye open.'

They waited, carefully scrutinizing the ground ahead but seeing little amiss. Down in the ruins someone fired the odd shot but the Indians did not return the fire. Locker found himself getting bored and bored men became careless. To stay alert the pair made idle conversation, just a few terse sentences but it helped keep them more conscious of their surroundings.

'What do you make of Avery and the others?' Frolech asked.

'Damned if I know. Lindsay might know more than he's telling us but this is a mighty odd place to be meeting friendly strangers. I'll take a bet, though, that that nice little girl down there with our horses is not really named Smith. Avery was too quick to hang that moniker on her and she nearly forgot when she introduced herself to me. There's something odd about that crew. Drysdale seems scared to death and Avery only seems worried about getting back his horse. Unless he's hoping to run away, a horse won't be a lot of use to him right now.'

Frolech spent a moment or two studying the ground in front of their position before replying. 'Drysdale looks ready to take off on foot. A man that scared is likely to panic and do anythin'. He's about as tough as custard and twice as yeller.'

Among the ruins, Avery tried a precautionary shot at some bushes that briefly appeared to be moving in strange directions but there was no evidence that he had done any execution. No shots came in reply and it seemed that in the midday heat both sides had taken time out of the fighting.

Frolech and Locker were feeling the heat and were regretting that they had not taken any water with them. Monotony was beginning to set in and despite good intentions about staying alert both found themselves half dozing.

Suddenly Locker shook himself out of his lethargy and whispered to his companion, 'We have company up the hill to the right.'

'I can't see anything. Are you sure?'

'Can you see a bunch of weeds about a hundred and fifty yards away, just near that cream-coloured rock?'

'I can. So what?'

'A few minutes ago it was back near that scrubby little cedar. Bushes sometimes spread but I never saw one travel as fast as that one. I reckon there's an Apache wrapped up in it somewhere.'

Frolech swore under his breath and wriggled around at right angles, taking care not to show himself to the concealed warrior. He found a narrow slit between the rocks from where he could aim his rifle without pushing the muzzle through. 'I'll have to judge this right because that varmint will be layin' as flat as a lizard and if I don't just skim the dirt, my shot will go over him from this angle.'

It seemed like ages before the big rifle boomed out but the bushes rolled sideways and Locker caught a brief glimpse of an arm thrown up above the weeds as the slug struck home.

'Nice shooting, Herman. If that Injun ain't dead, he'll be feeling mighty sick.'

But it was no time for congratulations. Another Indian with bushes attached to him jumped to his feet and ran in an attempt to bypass the two white men. Locker's Spencer spoke then, and the running man crashed down in a heap, dropping his rifle as he fell.

'Two less for us to worry about,'

71

Frolech muttered. 'Today's little dis-
agreement has cost them varmints fairly
dear.'

'That's what worries me, Herman.
Most tribes would call it quits after the
number they have already lost. There's
something special holding them here.'

No other Apaches seemed ready to
run the gauntlet but night was only a
few hours away and they would not be
such easy targets then.

Locker was worried. 'We're trying to
hold too wide a front. If I remember
rightly, this valley narrows a couple of
hundred yards further upstream. I
reckon we should leave the ruins and go
back up the river so we're fighting on a
much narrower front.'

'Getting back there and findin' the
right place to hole up could be tricky,'
Frolech said doubtfully.

'We don't have a choice, Herman.
They'll get around us in the dark if we
don't.'

7

Lindsay, Avery and Drysdale were looking ahead of them when they heard a flurry of shots and saw Locker sprinting downhill towards them. A couple of bullets kicked up dust around him as he crossed the exposed area but he managed to reach more sheltered ground without injury. The crack of Frolech's rifle announced that he had found a target among the Apaches but the shooter could not be sure that his bullet had struck home. No warrior presented himself as another target and again the defenders' rifles fell silent.

Locker eventually crawled into the sheltering ruins and acquainted those there of the impending peril. None disagreed with him but he felt he had to check before making final plans. He had not been told but assumed that Drysdale was Avery's guide. 'How well do you know the lay of the land further up the river?' he asked.

Drysdale replied warily, 'I know it a bit. When I was here with Shelby, I did a bit of dealing with the locals for supplies. I remember that a greaser named Ramirez had a big pumpkin patch back about two hundred yards or so upstream and then the gorge got narrow and too rocky fir anything to grow.'

'Were the locals friendly?'

'Some was, some wasn't but we got a few supplies from 'em. Why are you askin'? Ain't no locals here now so it don't matter much.'

There was a hard edge to Locker's voice as he said, 'I don't know what game you're playing but I do know that there were no locals in this village when Shelby came through — not live ones anyway. The Lipans had wiped out this village the day before. Shelby's men found a lot of tortured corpses but there was no one left alive.'

'That ain't right. I knew a few of the folks here.'

'It's right. I knew a few of Shelby's men who came back to Texas. They all spoke of what happened here. If you knew folks here it's because you were here before Shelby.'

'What if I was? That ain't no crime.'

At this point Avery interrupted. 'What are you driving at, Locker? This is no time for silly arguments.'

'It was a bit before my time,' Locker told him, 'but I heard this village was wiped out because a gang of scalp hunters had been using it as a supply base.'

The Pinkerton man gestured downstream and said scornfully, 'So what? The scalp hunters are still here. There's a heap of them not far away, or has that slipped your attention?'

'For your information, Avery, scalp hunters were white men who killed Indians and traded their scalps for money to the Mexican government. They would even murder Mexicans too if the hair looked right. If there's a lower trade than that, I've yet to see it. I reckon you've hired yourself a former scalp hunter for a guide. This *hombre* will draw Injuns like a magnet if they know who he is.'

Avery wheeled around to face Drysdale, his face flushed with anger. 'Is he right? Are you a scalp hunter?'

'No, I ain't,' the other protested. 'It ain't legal now. That was twelve years ago. You wanted someone to guide you here and I did that. What happened years ago, don't count now.'

'Those Apaches aren't after us,' Locker said angrily. 'They're after you. You probably thought the army had chased them all away or that they had forgotten you. Somehow, though, they knew you were back in Mexico. That's why you are so scared.'

Avery suddenly remembered. 'Tomás, that half-breed kid we hired. You reckoned he was careless, Drysdale, showing lights at night and smoke in the mornings. He was signalling to the Apaches.'

Lindsay said quietly, 'You're going real well, Avery. So far you seem to have

76

recruited one spy and one man who is drawing a big heap of trouble on us. Then just to complicate things, you bring a girl into this mess. Do you even know whose side she's on? I reckon you and I need to have a little talk.'

'I'm not the only one needs to explain things,' Avery said defensively. 'I am here hired by a private client and I happen to be looking for her father. What the hell are you doing here?'

'I was hired by some of a man's business associates to bring him back from Mexico. It seems he's in some trouble down here and they want him back.'

'So doesn't it seem like one big coincidence that we're both here in the one place at the one time?' The disbelief in the detective's tone was plain.

'If I were a betting man, I would be betting that maybe we are both looking for the same man. What do you think, Avery?'

'I was never told that other parties were involved. Miss Dixon told me that her old man was acting alone in all of this.'

'Maybe she didn't know. And on the subject of women, I suppose there's a good reason for bringing a girl down here, but right now I find it hard to think of one.' Lindsay made no effort to disguise the disapproval in his voice.

While the two leaders were airing their mutual suspicions, Locker slipped away and returned to where Jenny waited with the horses. He explained that he needed a drink from one of the water canteens and would take the rest up to Frolech.

'I'm glad you came along,' Jenny told him. 'I don't dare leave these horses, but I saw a Mexican on a mule a few minutes ago. He was looking down from the top of that big hill on our right.'

'Are you sure it was a Mexican and not an Apache?'

'He looked like some of the Mexicans I saw in Eagle Pass. He had a black beard and wore a cheap straw sombrero. He looked a villainous type and dropped out of sight quickly. I don't know what he was intending but I was thinking I should have taken a shot at him.'

'You wouldn't hit him from here with a pistol so it's a good thing you didn't try. He might have shot back.'

'I couldn't see if he had a gun.'

'If he didn't, he must have had some pretty well-armed friends nearby. This ain't healthy country for a man with no gun.' Then Locker changed the subject. 'Lindsay and Avery are figuring things out but when it gets dark, we'll be going further up the canyon so the Apaches can't get round us in the night. I don't know what you folks are doing here but it looks like we'll be stuck with each other. Even without the Apaches, things could get mighty serious around here in the next day or so. Could you tell me what's going on?'

Jenny hesitated and almost weakened but then shook her head. 'I'm sorry, Bill, but I can't. There's too much at stake. I promised Phil Avery that I would do as he said.'

Locker slung the canteen over his shoulder. 'That's fair enough. I'll just make a final check with our two big chiefs and tell them about your Mexican. Then I'll head back to Frolech. If all goes well, we'll catch up with you further up the canyon tonight. Take care of yourself, Jenny.'

★   ★   ★

A few scattered shots greeted Locker as he returned to where Frolech waited but the scout's luck held. The rifleman eagerly took the canteen he was offered and swallowed a couple of deep drinks before replacing the stopper.' I needed that,' he muttered. 'I'm so dry, my hide's crackin'.

'When it gets dark, we're all moving back up the gorge to a safer position where the Apaches can't creep around us. Lindsay will fire a shot from the ruins when all the others are safely away. Chances are that the Apaches will just think it's a nervous sentry.'

Frolech licked his lips nervously. 'I hope they don't wait too long because as soon as the light gets bad, those varmints might start moving in on us. They can be hard enough to see in broad daylight.'

'Before I came back I was talking to Jenny. She said she saw a Mexican up on the rimrock. Looks like Dixon's kidnappers are starting to arrive. I found out something else too. That Drysdale *hombre* is an old scalp hunter. Seems he thought it might be safe to venture back here but somehow the Apaches know he's back. I reckon he's the one that brought all this extra trouble on us.'

'And where does that girl fit into all this?'

'I'm guessing she's Dixon's daughter but it's only a guess. In case you haven't noticed, Herman, no sonofabitch has told me a hell of a lot about what's going on. We have a prime target for the Apaches, another *hombre* who is worried about losing his horse, and a girl who's acting mighty mysterious. Then we have Lindsay who don't say any more than he has to. I hope you ain't keeping secrets too.'

'You can rest easy there. I've worked with Lindsay long enough to know it's best not to ask too many questions. He tells me all I need to know about the work and I don't want to know what goes on behind the scenes.'

Sheltering from the sun as much as they could, the pair settled down to wait. Gradually the shadow cast by the canyon wall spread across the narrow valley. Both men knew that even before the sun had set, the gathering shadows would hinder visibility and give the Apaches the opportunity to start another assault.

The change from light, to shade, to almost total darkness came swiftly and the pair on the hill waited anxiously for the signal that the others had moved out. Now was the time when imagination could take over and every vague shadow, bush or rock could easily be mistaken for a crouching warrior. Sight was deceptive and now they kept silent listening for the faintest noises that could indicate nearby enemies.

The report of a rifle from among the ruins came at last.

Locker whispered to Frolech. 'Time to go. Let's hope we can get away from here before the Indians start moving around us and maybe cut us off from the others.'

8

Locker led the way, with Frolech a few yards behind him. They moved as slowly and as silently as they could but some sound was inevitable. Every few paces the scout would pause and listen for short, tension-filled intervals. He estimated that they were halfway to their objective when he heard the first, very faint sound. Had a wind been blowing, he would have dismissed it as a few leaves on a bush being stirred, or possibly the noise made by a small animal, but instinct told him it was something far more deadly. His first inclination was to warn Frolech but he knew that to do so would betray his position. Instead he crouched and waited.

The attack came suddenly, marked first by a sharply indrawn breath, then by a rush of movement. Instinctively Locker threw up his carbine. There was the clang of steel on steel and the weapon was almost torn from his grasp as a tomahawk struck the upraised barrel. Simultaneously an Apache war cry echoed along the canyon.

Neither protagonist could see the other properly and it was only by luck that Locker struck something solidly when he lashed out with the butt of his carbine. He could not tell how effective the blow had been but heard the sound of someone falling back into the bushes. The time for silence was over.

'They're on to us, Herman. Head up the canyon as quick as you can.'

The fallen Apache was calling to his companions and Locker was tempted to chance a shot in his direction but decided it was better if he did not give any more lurking warriors a gun flash for an aiming point.

Frolech's boots clattered on rocks and the sound of a person smashing his way through bushes advertised that the rifleman had no intention of trying to fight in the dark. It was pointless to be silent any longer.

Locker swung his rifle butt again and must have caught the warrior as he struggled to his feet. Again the blow landed heavily and the bushes rustled once more as a body fell back among them. Wheeling about, stumbling over uneven ground and breaking through bushes, the scout followed his companion.

'Don't shoot!' Frolech called because he knew that they were approaching the others and there was every excuse for an itchy trigger finger.

Behind them in the darkness an Apache fired but the combination of darkness and distance meant that the shot was wasted.

Lindsay called from a few yards ahead. 'Over here. Come this way.'

Frolech cursed as he tripped over the log behind which his boss was sheltering. Guided by the sounds, Locker quickly joined them. Before he had a chance to say a word a series of shots and muzzle flashes told him that

Drysdale was firing in panic into the darkness. This attracted the attention of the Apaches and a few rifles fired back. A couple of bullets came close enough to convince the white men that there were healthier places to be.

'Stop shooting,' Avery shouted. 'You're giving away our position and drawing fire on us.'

Frolech was even less diplomatic. 'You fire one more shot,' he threatened, 'and I'll bust your skull with my rifle butt.'

'They're comin'.' Drysdale almost shrieked in his terror. 'Don't you know they're shootin' at us?'

'Those shots came from a fair way away. It was your shooting that attracted them,' Lindsay said quietly.

Locker explained. 'I think they had a scout out looking for us. We must have nearly stumbled into each other in the dark. If there had been more scouts, they would have joined in the shooting.'

'Everyone,' said Lindsay, 'keep under cover and keep quiet.'

They listened but in the minutes that dragged by, heard nothing to indicate an impending attack.

Locker crept back to where Jenny was holding the horses in a grove of pine trees. Guided by the faint sounds made by the horses, he groped his way in the gloom. Remembering too that the girl had a revolver, and having no desire to be mistaken for an Apache, he whispered, 'Jenny, it's Bill — don't shoot.'

A very frightened, soft voice whispered, 'Over here.'

Locker moved quietly to where the girl stood, still faithfully holding the horses. 'I'm just checking. Are you all right?'

'That depends upon how seriously you rate being scared almost to death. I think they could be behind us.'

'What makes you think that?'

'I am certain I heard horses, and the horses here have been acting as though something strange is about.'

It was useless peering into the darkness among the trees but Locker was not prepared to dismiss such disquieting news as the product of an overactive imagination. 'Wait here,' he whispered. 'I'll see what I can find out. If you hear me call out, run back to the others. If all is well, I'll whistle once, very softly as I come back. I'll leave my carbine with you. If you have to use it, just cock the hammer and fire. Push down the trigger guard and load in another cartridge. But you still have to cock the hammer to shoot. This isn't like a Henry or a Winchester that cocks itself. Now remember, if I'm coming back. I'll whistle.'

Seconds later Locker had blended into the darkness of the trees. He moved slowly, placing his feet down carefully to avoid making any unnecessary noise. But, much as he tried to suppress them, some sounds were unavoidable. In one place he blundered into a low tree branch and shortly afterwards stumbled over a large rock. It did nothing for his peace of mind to think that enemies could be sitting silently in the gloom just waiting for him to move into killing range. He guessed he had crept about a hundred yards into the trees when a stray current of wind brought a faint smell to his nostrils: horses. Jenny had been right.

But where were the riders?

He halted and listened. Bushes were rustling and a restless stamping was coming from somewhere to his left. It took him several minutes to move the next couple of paces but eventually he could just discern a clearing ahead. The light was marginally better and his straining eyes detected movement. He could see the vague outlines of two horses at the edge of the clearing but the idea occurred to him that the animals could be bait for a trap.

While Locker was pondering his next move, one of the horses shook itself and saddle flaps rattled, indicating that these were not Indian ponies. Relief flooded through him as Locker suddenly remembered the horses that Avery and Drysdale had lost. Taking a chance, he spoke softly so the animals would not take fright at his approach and walked quietly towards them. Much to his relief they did not move away although they did raise their heads at his approach.

The surprise came when he was feeling around in the dark for the trailing reins that he was sure would have stopped at least one horse. Not finding them, he carefully stroked the nearest animal and felt around its head, expecting to find a missing or broken bridle. Instead he found the reins fastened to a low tree branch. A quick check showed the second animal similarly secured.

The hair rose on the back of Locker's neck when he realized that someone had placed the horses there. Again, his first reaction was that they were bait for a trap but there was no sudden blast of a weapon or an Apache war cry. Puzzled and more than a little nervous, he set out to lead the horses back to the others.

When he reckoned he was close enough, he gave a soft whistle. Jenny's voice answered. 'Is that you, Bill?'

'Sure is and I've found a couple of lost horses. I reckon Avery can stop his belly-aching now.'

They held a whispered conversation. Jenny was a little disappointed that her pony had not been found. To relieve her monotony, Locker volunteered to hold the horses while the girl went to inform Avery of the discovery.

The Pinkerton man came hurrying back. 'Jenny said you found these horses tied up. What's been taken?'

'How would I know? What was on your horse that had you in such a lather anyway?'

Avery ignored the question and rushed to his horse, cursing as he unbuckled the saddle-bags in the dark. Lifting the flap, he felt inside and in a wondering tone said, 'I *don't* believe it. There was a lot of money in here that still seems to be here. I won't know until daylight when it's light enough to see but I think it's all there. That can't be right.'

Locker could only venture the opinion that the person who found the horses had been unable to check the contents of the saddle-bags and had hidden the horses, hoping to collect them later.

Avery detached the bags and slung them over his shoulder declaring as he did so, 'I don't know what went on this afternoon but from now on I don't let these bags out of my sight.'

'You have Jenny to thank for getting your stuff back,' Locker reminded him.

'I also have Jenny to thank for getting me into this mess,' Avery replied bitterly.

Locker was tired of mysteries. 'It's about time someone told me what's going on around here. Why are two different parties of *Americanos* at this one little place at the one time?'

The detective muttered in a harsh tone. 'That's exactly what I intend to ask Ike Lindsay.'

9

Lindsay was not in the best of moods. His carefully laid plans were in jeopardy thanks to Avery and the others. It was with great difficulty that he restrained himself when the detective demanded to know the real reason he was in the Sabinas Valley.

'You don't have the right to ask me anything, Avery,' he growled. 'Why are you bird-dogging me? Who's paying you?'

'I'm not following you at all, Lindsay. I am working for a private client and I don't give two hoots in hell what you're doing here. My work has nothing to do with you and I would be deleriously happy if you should go away and let me do it.'

Lindsay scratched his chin and said cautiously, 'You wouldn't be looking for a mining engineer named Dixon by any chance?'

The sharp intake of the detective's breath was confirmation enough of Lindsay's theory. 'What makes you think that?' Even the question itself was unconvincing.

'I'll guess a little further, Avery. You are here to ransom Dixon from a part-time bandit and full-time member of the Mexican government who calls himself Manuel Estrada. That's why you were so all-fired anxious about your horse. You thought you'd lost the ransom money.'

'You're right. The girl is his daughter. She raised the money somehow and hired Pinkertons to do the deal. How did you know?'

'Because I was hired by people who will remain nameless to do the same doggone thing. Seems like Estrada sent out two ransom demands to addresses that only Dixon must have given him. Our bandit friend is having two bites of the cherry and he has arranged for us to both be here at the same time.'

'He probably thought one letter

might not have brought results,' Avery speculated.

'He knew because we had to reply through a padre in a place called Nacimiento. It seems he did not want to be seen as being too closely involved. If too big an incident happens at government level he can claim that the padre was the instigator and probably have him rubbed out.'

'That would be no loss. I hate those sanctimonious blood-suckers. Everyone knows they're behind a lot of Mexico's problems.'

'There's some would argue about that but what I want to know is why you brought Jenny Dixon along.'

'It wasn't my choice. She's paying the bills and is the only one who can positively identify her father. I objected but head office overrode me.'

Lindsay shook his head in disgust but he had more pressing matters on his mind. 'Right now we can forget about any bandits because chances are those Indians will overrun us first. You did a mighty fine job of recruiting help, a scalp hunter that the Apaches want and another *hombre* who just happened to be working for them.'

'I didn't get much choice,' Avery said defensively. 'I was in Denver and was suddenly ordered by telegram to go to Eagle Pass and organize this little expedition. You might not have noticed but there seems a rare shortage of suitable people in this particular hole in the ground. I had to make do with the guides I could get. I wouldn't have been able to hire Drysdale if he'd known that the Apaches have such long memories. The sneaky bastard pretended that he had been a government scout. I wonder if it's not too late to hand him over to the Indians.'

'While the idea has a certain appeal, I couldn't go along with that,' Lindsay declared. 'And it's too damn late. By now the Lipans are looking to settle accounts for a few of their men that we let daylight through today.'

Locker had rejoined Jenny as she held the horses and fought to stay awake. 'I'll take over here. You try to get a bit of sleep,' he told her. Untying a heavy coat from behind the cantle of his saddle, he passed it to her. 'You'd better put this on under your serape or you'll be too cold to sleep on this hard ground.'

'What about you?'

'I won't be doing too much sleeping; I'll look after the horses.'

Jenny started feeling around for a level place clear of the horses to stretch out but asked as she did so, 'What's going to happen in the morning, Bill?'

Locker had a pretty fair notion but preferred not to say. Instead, he shrugged his shoulders and replied vaguely, 'Who knows? Sometimes things turn out different to what they look. Now try to get some sleep.'

Lindsay came around half an hour later and in whispered tones told

Locker the situation. The scout had suspected something was strange but had never envisaged that two groups, unbeknown to each other, would be on the same errand at the same time.

'This Estrada character has planned things pretty well,' Lindsay explained. He had Dixon write identical letters to both parties. Chances are, he thought one ransom demand might go astray or be ignored. Turns out he hit the jackpot.'

'How much does Jenny know about her father's business?' asked Locker.

'Avery finally admitted she's Dixon's daughter. She raised the ransom and hired Pinkertons to do the job but insisted upon coming along because she could identify her father. Avery wasn't keen on that arrangement but had to do as his bosses told him. Right now, though, our problem is with those Apaches. Do you reckon they'll attack tonight?'

'They might but night attacks are a problem to plan. Even the Lipans can't see in the dark any better than we can and no one can be completely silent on a dark night. The advantage is with the man sitting still and listening. Odds are, they'll attack at first light.'

'How good are our chances?'

Locker thought a while before replying. 'The numbers might be on their side but we have better guns and can do them a lot of damage. It's not hopeless. If we don't lose too many too soon, we have a chance. Of course we don't know what Drysdale will do. If he fights, the extra gun will make a big difference but if he don't there'll only be four of us and Jenny. That girl's worth a dozen Drysdales. Avery should never have hired that yellow sonofa-bitch.'

'Well, he has and we are stuck with him. I'm going back to the others. Keep a sharp eye out here.'

A couple of times in the hours that followed a panic-stricken Drysdale fired into the darkness as he imagined an Apache stealing towards him. No shots came in reply but the silence only made the darkness more menacing. Finally dawn was a red streak in the east and visibility started to improve.

Locker's experience told him that an attack would soon be coming and he was about to wake Jenny when he saw a vague shape moving towards them through the sheltering pine trees. He snapped the Spencer to his shoulder and squinted down the barrel, remaining partially concealed behind a large tree trunk.

The intruder noted the movement and called out in heavily accented English, 'Don't shoot, señor. I am a friend.'

'If you are a friend, come in very slowly. I'll kill you at the first sign I don't like. Come in alone and keep your hands where I can see them.'

'I am alone. I will come in carefully. I am unarmed.'

A Mexican astride a brown mule emerged from cover and, holding his right hand high to show that it was empty, he steered his mount towards the scout. He wore a cheap straw sombrero and was swathed in a faded serape from which emerged legs in cheap white cotton trousers. His feet were in scuffed sandals and his overall appearance was that of a none-too-prosperous Mexican peasant. His lined face had the broad cheekbones of an Indian and was framed by untidy, grey-streaked hair and a roughly trimmed beard. There was a scar across his forehead and two narrow, dark eyes peered through slitted lids. They took in everything about them and reflected a sharp mind behind a very ordinary appearance.

Apart from a tomahawk under the saddle strings securing a blanket roll, the newcomer did not appeared to be armed although the voluminous serape could conceal any number of weapons.

Locker was taking no chances. Knowing that Jenny would be awake, he called to her. 'Jenny, get Lindsay or Avery here quick.' Then he commanded, 'Get off that mule real easy, *amigo*. And then get your hands up. You have a few questions to answer.'

'Be careful with that gun, *señor*. I mean you no harm. I do not carry any weapons.'

Locker pointed to the mule. 'There's a tomahawk there in easy reach.'

The newcomer smiled, displaying a mouth with broken and missing teeth. 'That is only for cutting firewood or making a shelter when I am travelling. I am here to help you, not to cause trouble.'

'Who are you?'

'My name is Domingo. What I do is not your worry.'

'Are you one of Estrada's men?'

'I am not but I know him. Everyone here does.'

'Did you find those horses and bring them back?'

'I did. I saw part of your fight with the Indians yesterday so I knew who owned them.'

'You weren't tempted to keep them, 'specially when you knew what one horse was carrying?'

The Mexican said simply, 'I am not a thief.'

Lindsay arrived, accompanied by Jenny. The scout informed him that the newcomer had returned two of the lost horses and his boss gave vent to his curiousity. He looked about suspiciously before asking none too politely, 'What are you doing here? Are you looking for a reward for returning the horses? Don't you know the Apaches might attack at any moment?'

Domingo's face twisted into his version of a smile and his dark eyes seemed to narrow even more. 'I want no reward. The Indians will not attack. I saw them leave this area during the night.'

Locker was the first to recover from his surprise. 'That don't make sense. They had us in a big heap of trouble. Why would they leave when our party has a man they want and we have killed a couple of their warriors?'

The newcomer replied, 'They know they would not be able to kill you all before the odds against them became too great.'

'I don't believe that,' Lindsay declared.

'You will when Estrada gets here. He has many men and is not far away.'

'Then what are you doing here, Domingo?' Locker was puzzled.

'I am here trying to save your lives. I was a friend of Señor Dixon. Estrada means to kill you all and take the ransom money.'

'You said you 'were' a friend of Dixon. Have you fallen out or disagreed about something?' But the question was no sooner out of his mouth than Locker realized the implication of the Mexican's statement.

Speaking this time in Spanish, and hoping that Locker understood, the Mexican said quietly, 'What I am trying to say, is that Dixon is dead. Estrada cannot free a dead man.'

Shocked by the news, Locker began to question the newcomer more deeply but the rest of his party were becoming impatient.

'What's he saying?' Lindsay demanded. 'Why isn't he speaking English?'

Aware that Jenny was in earshot, Locker told him, 'I'll tell you in a minute. Meanwhile we had better start thinking of getting away from here.'

'You must hurry,' Domingo insisted, speaking again in English. 'Estrada already must be very close. He means to steal the ransom and to kill you all.'

10

'I came here to get Dixon.' Lindsay said. 'I don't intend to be scared away by some Mexican tramp. I'm sure that Avery and Miss Dixon feel the same way. I wouldn't believe a word this fellow says. What sort of a story was he giving you in Spanish? I'm not sure you translated to us all that was said.'

'We had a short talk but that has nothing to do with what's about to happen. The most important thing is that he was trying to find a way of breaking the news gently to Jenny,' said Locker. 'But I don't reckon there is any easy way. He reckons that Dixon is dead, thinks he died of pneumonia.' He turned to the girl whose face had suddenly gone pale. 'I'm sorry, Jenny, but Domingo here told me that your father died about a week ago.'

There was a small gasp of disbelief.

For a second she closed her eyes and shook her head. Tears welled up and when she finally looked at Locker, she said in a small, shocked voice, 'Are you sure this is true?'

'I'm pretty sure. This man has no reason to lie.'

'Yes he does,' Avery announced loudly as he suddenly strode onto the scene. The others had not noticed his arrival. 'He could be in cahoots with those Indians, selling us out in return for the ransom money, or he could be working for a rival bandit who has heard of the deal and is trying to beat Estrada to the money. He's in an almighty hurry to get us out of here and most likely some of his more unsavoury friends are waiting somewhere down the trail in ambush.'

Anger momentarily flashed in Domingo's eyes. 'You are wrong, señor. I knew Dixon when he was a captive of Estrada. We formed a friendship and I was there when he wrote the two ransom letters. I posted them and took your replies back to Estrada. When he died I buried him.'

'So you did work for Estrada,' Lindsay accused.

'I was never a member of his band but I spoke English and Estrada sometimes conscripted me when he was questioning Señor Dixon. I do not approve of kidnapping or ransom but it is better than outright murder. I was trying to keep Dixon from being killed. His only chance of staying alive was to make him too valuable to kill but I am afraid that my efforts were to no avail. I could have stolen your money yesterday if I was after it. You seem to have forgotten that I brought back your horses and the money. What other proof of my good intentions do you need?'

'You speak pretty fancy for a poor Mexican,' Avery said as he glared at the stranger. 'I think you're in disguise. If you know what's good for you, you'll tell us what's going on.'

'What is good for all of you is more to the point, señor. I am an educated man but I assure you that I am not a wealthy one. I am doing this out of friendship with Señor Dixon and to prevent more killing. You must believe me. You are in great danger. Get out of here while you can.'

'It's not all that simple,' Lindsay told him. 'I need more than just your word. I need proof.'

'And so do I,' Avery affirmed.

'You are likely to die before you get it. For the young lady's sake I ask you to reconsider. There is not much time. I must go because if Estrada knows I have been here, he will kill me also.'

'I believe you, Domingo, but we could run straight into those Apaches if we go now,' Locker said. 'They won't be far away.'

Domingo turned, and mounted his mule. 'I have done all that I can. I can wait no longer. I know where the Apaches are likely to be waiting for you and can show you a path that will avoid them.' He said to Locker, 'I know you are a scout. I saw you before when the *Americano* soldiers last crossed the border.'

'I don't remember you,' Locker admitted.

The Mexican gave a rueful smile. 'We did not meet and in a small village here I am just another person in the street. When I leave here, I will leave a clear trail that you can follow. It will be your best chance of reaching safety. Try to talk sense into the others.'

Avery stepped forward and grabbed the mule's bridle just as Domingo was about to ride away. 'You are not going anywhere, Greaser. I don't know what game you're playing but I want a few more answers from you.'

'Let him go,' Locker ordered. 'We have some mighty quick decisions to make and we can't waste time arguing about this man's motives. I believe him. You should be damn grateful that he got your money back. He had nothing to gain by coming here. We should be deciding what we're going to do about the situation. What do you reckon, Lindsay?'

'I don't know. This could be some sort of trap. Estrada could be planning a doublecross and this man might be reporting back to him.'

'It would hardly suit Estrada's plans to have us prepared to fight him when he can capture us by means of a trick at no risk to himself,' Locker insisted. 'If Domingo worked for Estrada, he would not have returned the horses and money. There's no better proof than that.'

'I want to see some evidence of the true situation regarding Dixon. Pinkertons want more than the word of some Mexican peasant.' But beneath the blustering tone, Avery's voice was showing the first signs of doubt.

'And so do I,' Jenny said firmly. 'I won't abandon my father on the say-so of some wandering Mexican.'

Lindsay was convinced. 'Looks like we stay, Locker.'

The scout turned to the man on the mule. 'Thanks, *amigo*. Good luck.' Then to Avery he said, 'Let go of that bridle. There's nothing to be gained by stopping this man.'

Reluctantly the detective released his hold and glared after the Mexican as he rode away. Then he shrugged his shoulders and turned to the others as though all inspiration had left him.

Given Avery's apparent indecision, Lindsay quietly assumed control of the party. He had the horses prepared to travel and the group moved to a spot where they were backed against the canyon wall and protected on the other sides by trees and rocks. Locker volunteered to scout a short way upstream; Frolech would do the same downstream. The others took up a defensive position that would be fairly strong in daylight but difficult to hold when night fell. None dared speculate where they would be when the day ended.

Locker stole out on foot, moving quietly through the trees to a point where he could see open country beyond. If Domingo was right, Estrada would not be far away. A few minutes later the

Mexican's warnings proved to be accurate. Half a mile to the north-west, he could see a long bare slope. A line of horsemen was moving down it in single file on a steep path. The morning sun was glinting ominously on the many weapons the riders were carrying. Abandoning all caution, he turned and ran back to where the others were waiting.

As he panted up to the defences, he noted that Frolech was already back from his patrol.

All could read the urgency in the scout's actions and the questions came thick and fast as he sat on a log to regain his breath. 'They're coming,' he gasped.

'How many?' Lindsay demanded.

'Looks like a couple of dozen. I didn't stop to make a proper count but there's plenty to go round.'

11

'How do we handle this?' Locker asked Lindsay.

'We don't shoot until we see if what that Mexican told us is true. If Dixon is still alive, we don't want to jeopardize his chances. We'll try to stop them at a distance until we can see the true situation — that's provided they don't come in shooting.'

Frolech carefully checked the sights on his rifle. 'We don't know what this Estrada character looks like but if any shootin' starts, I'll try to pick off the one givin' orders.'

'That's fine by me,' his boss told him, 'but wait till I give the word.'

Locker had his field glasses trained up the valley. 'They're just coming into view now,' he said. 'I can see what looks like an American in a brown coat and hat riding up front with the leading group.'

'I told you that Domingo character was lying,' Avery declared.

'He looks like a tall, thin fella with a black beard,' Locker continued. 'It might be an idea if Jenny has a look through these glasses.'

Hope came back into the girl's face as she eagerly accepted the binoculars. Making no effort to keep the excitement out of her voice, she told the others, 'I recognize my father's coat and hat, I can't get a good look at his face but I think it's him.'

'Time we stopped them,' Lindsay announced. 'Herman, put a shot about twenty yards ahead of those riders. Then when they stop I'll get Locker to call to them. There's no way we want all that crowd around us during negotiations.'

Frolech's rifle boomed and a spurt of red dust arose ahead of the advancing riders. As they halted in apparent confusion, Locker emerged from cover, waved his arms and called out in Spanish, 'Stop there and send in one man, preferably someone who speaks English.'

The horsemen milled about for a while as they discussed the situation and then finally a villainous-looking individual rode out of the group and advanced at a brisk walk. He was adorned with a variety of weapons and sat easily on a wiry, sorrel pony. His face bore a contemptuous grin as he halted his mount a few yards from the party and leaned down on his pelican-bill saddle horn.

Avery walked over to Locker. 'I want to ask that greaser a few questions as well, so try to keep the conversation in English.'

'Fair enough,' the scout agreed, 'but don't make yourself too much of a target. I still reckon Estrada intends to kill us if he gets the chance.'

The detective was not convinced. 'I think that Domingo character was playing games with us. He said that Dixon was dead and yet I can see him over there.'

'Are you sure? See what Jenny Dixon thinks.'

'Look at the excitement on her face, Locker. She can see it's her father.'

The Mexican sat patiently on his horse in front of Locker but looked beyond him as though already counting the number of potential enemies in the background.

The scout asked if he spoke English but the man shook his head. In Spanish he explained that none of his comrades had sufficient English knowledge to conduct negotiations. He admitted that he was not Estrada but spoke on his leader's behalf.

Locker suspected that the man was fluent in English but hoped to overhear any unguarded comments as the Americans discussed the message he brought. It was a simple one: give Estrada the money and he would release Dixon. He let it be known also that his leader was aware that both parties to whom the ransom demands had been sent, had combined their forces. The hostage taker would not release his victim for less then ten thousand dollars.

When he heard the offer translated, Avery said disdainfully, 'Does Estrada think we're that stupid? No money changes hands until Dixon is free.'

The Mexican frowned when he heard that but such an answer was predictable. It was Lindsay who came up with a compromise. 'Let's meet halfway between both sides and make the exchange.'

'That's not a good idea,' Locker told him. 'There's nothing to stop Estrada shooting the man who delivers the money as soon as he hands it over.'

'I'm prepared to take the risk,' Lindsay announced.

Locker turned to the rider and relayed details of the conversation, although he was sure that the man already knew. Just as the emissary was about to return to his leader, the scout casually asked which of the distant group was Estrada.

'That is not your business,' the man said sharply, and then rode away.

Anxiously they watched the Mexicans

cluster around the messenger as though planning their next move.

Jenny left cover and walked to Locker's side. She handed him the binoculars and said, 'I can't really be sure that's my father. The build and the clothes are right but I am thinking of what Domingo said. I am going to take off my sombrero and wave. Even at this distance I think my father would recognize me. If he waves back it will probably be him. I want you to watch closely through the glasses and tell me exactly what he does.'

Removing her hat and shaking out her long hair, Jenny began waving enthusiastically. It caught the attention of Estrada's men. There was a brief pause and the man in the brown coat, as though prompted, began waving back with great energy. He was still partially obscured by the other riders but there was no doubt as to his enthusiasm.

'Looks like he's mighty pleased to see you,' Locker observed.

'I want you to be very sure, Bill.

Which hand is he waving?'

'He's waving his right hand. You can see it over that group of riders that are milling about.'

In a voice laden with sadness and disappointment, Jenny said softly, 'That's not my father. He had a bad shoulder wound from the war and can't lift his right arm above shoulder level. It can't possibly be him.'

'Are you sure of that?'

'I wish I was not but I know now that Domingo told the truth. That is not my father. He is dead.'

At any other time Locker might have tried to say something sympathetic but now he had other priorities. 'We'd best get back to the others. Things are going to get very lively around here in a couple of minutes.'

Avery was waiting impatiently for them. 'How do we arrange paying this ransom?'

'We don't. That's not Jenny's father. She knows that for sure.'

'What do we do now?' the detective muttered.

'We have to fight,' Lindsay told him sharply. 'There's no other way.'

As though waiting for just that time, Frolech came up with a plan that was murderously simple. He suggested that he shoot Estrada in the hope that the other side might lose heart without their leader. The problem, however, was that none of them could identify their target. Some of the Mexicans were well dressed and armed while others wore ragged clothes and were poorly equipped. It was logical that the leader would be one of the better-dressed group but it seemed that he was deliberately keeping a low profile as insurance against just such tactics as his intended victims were planning.

Peering through his field glasses Lindsay said, 'He could be one of about four men over there. They're all milling about and not really giving us a good look at any of them.'

'Forget about the men,' Locker said. 'Look for the best horse because you can bet Estrada will have it. We'll need to hurry. They'll be getting suspicious soon and it won't be long before they attack us.'

'I can see a nice dark brown horse, with a lot of silver on its bridle. See what you reckon, Locker. The rider has a red shirt.'

'I think you're right. Get Herman to knock over that sneaky sonofabitch and we'll see what happens then.'

Avery protested. 'But that will end all chances of negotiating our way out of this.'

'There never was a chance of that,' Locker said harshly. 'That treacherous skunk has intended to murder us all right from the start.'

'We shouldn't be firing the first shot,' the detective argued. 'It could cause legal problems later.'

In no mood for further argument, Lindsay snapped, 'There's no law here. Kill that man, Herman.'

Frolech had stayed undercover and now eased out his rifle barrel through a narrow gap in the weeds that concealed him. 'So you reckon Estrada's the one in the red shirt?'

'He'll do for a start,' Lindsay said grimly.

'There's their messenger coming again,' Avery said. 'Let's hear what he wants.'

The rider stopped about a hundred yards from them and called out in Spanish, 'Estrada wants to know why you are delaying.'

Locker was reluctant to commence hostilities by shooting the man, and shouted back, 'The deal's off. We know Dixon is dead. Tell Estrada to go home now or to come shooting.'

The emissary wheeled his horse and galloped away. The watchers saw him reach his comrades, heard the angry shout that arose and saw weapons being brandished. More ominously they began to form up as though they intended charging. The man in the red shirt remained in the background, moving constantly behind the other riders.

The scout was watching through his

field glasses as the attack was being prepared, so the report of Frolech's rifle took him by surprise. He saw a man on the ground. The horsemen were scattering but the man with the red shirt was still in his saddle.

Frolech cursed under his breath. As he reloaded he explained, 'That dang fool rode right in front of his boss just as I pulled the trigger. Serves him right. Now I have to get Estrada all over again.'

'Get ready,' Lindsay ordered with a calm that indicated he was no stranger to such situations. 'Nobody shoot until I give the word.'

The distant horsemen started spacing themselves widely in the hope that the bullet that missed one would not hit another. 'We can't stop them all,' Avery said softly. 'Some are bound to get through to us.'

Locker told him, 'See that low band of black volcanic rock about a hundred paces out? I saw that earlier. It has a lot of sharp edges on it and nobody would gallop a horse through it. The odd rider might try to jump it but most will turn towards the centre to go around it. That will mean a lot of riders will be coming around the end of those rocks and crowding up as they do. Their wide spacing will be gone and we can do them a lot of damage as they bunch up. Bring down a few horses and riders there and they'll all be in each other's way. Those in front will only be interested in not getting shot and any behind will have to come around the left of them to get at us. That will still make them good targets.'

Lindsay, who was listening from nearby, nodded his head in agreement. 'I think you're right, Locker. If we can do enough damage to them at that point, they might give up the idea, 'specially if we get Estrada.'

Avery was not so sure. 'I think they'll keep coming. I saw a few situations like this in the war.'

'These men are not soldiers,' Lindsay reminded him. 'They are bandits fighting for loot. They have no discipline.'

'I sure hope you're right,' said Frolech, 'because here they come.'

12

With wild yells, the horsemen urged their mounts into motion and surged foward in a widely spaced, ragged line. Some crouched low over their horses' necks, others stood in their stirrups brandishing guns and shouting defiance.

'Wait,' Lindsay cautioned. 'See if they turn away when they discover that patch of sharp rocks. If they do, then we'll have much better targets.'

Through his rifle sights, Locker sought out Estrada. He saw him briefly but the bandit chief had eased back his horse and another rider, travelling faster, cut in front of him.

Distance had foreshortened the width of the old lava bed and long grass had partially concealed it until the riders came close. Suddenly they saw it and there were shouts of alarm and much hauling on reins. One horse blundered into the black teeth showing through the ground. It staggered, managed another stride and fell. Another rider tried to jump the rocks but the barrier was too wide and the horse refused, sitting back on its haunches and almost sliding into the solidified lava. The rider frantically turned his pony at right angles and shouted a warning to others who had dropped behind. The horsemen turned to their left and urged their mounts around the end of the rocky patch. Turned side-on and all riding for the one point, they became a closely packed wall of horses.

'Now!' shouted Lindsay as he commenced firing into the mass of men and animals that even the poorest shot would be unlikely to miss.

Horses fell, some struck by bullets and others colliding with following animals as their riders tried to turn them away from the hail of lead. Men went down, either shot or dislodged in collisions, but at the other end of the line a few riders emerged unhindered and unscathed.

Locker cast aside his carbine, having fired all seven shots, and drew a revolver. A rider was bearing down on him, snapping pistol shots in his direction as he came. Gambling that the horseman's wild shots would most likely go astray, he sighted carefully on the front of the man's dirty shirt and squeezed the trigger. His target crashed from the saddle and the awkward way he fell indicated that he was unlikely to cause further trouble.

Frolech swung his empty rifle like a club and unhorsed another rider. Drysdale shot the man as he tried to rise.

Estrada's men were firing back and those now on foot were aiming carefully. A couple of bullets whined off the rock that sheltered Locker and he heard a grunt and a curse from Lindsay. Another rider seemed to have come from nowhere and the scout's attention was drawn away from his wounded boss. The horseman leaned low in his saddle and squinted at Locker along the barrel of his revolver.

But another of the defenders had seen him and fired first. The man reeled, dropped his gun and clung to the saddle horn as his mount wheeled away and bolted with him.

The firing began to slacken but a haze of gun-smoke hung around the defenders' position, partially obscuring their view of the battlefield. Never one to waste a bullet, Frolech peered through the smoke and shouted, 'They're fallin' back — keep shootin'.'

Avery crammed bullets into the magazine of his rifle. He halted, fired the couple of shots he had already loaded and re-commenced his task.

Drysdale's paralyzing fear of Apaches did not extend to Mexicans and he laid down a steady fire.

A light wind blew some of the smoke away and the defenders saw the ground before them dotted with dead horses and fallen men. A couple of wounded horses were still on their feet but unable to move. In the distance small groups of dismounted men and riders were helping wounded comrades towards cover.

'They're beaten,' Avery called.

Locker contradicted him. 'Like hell they are. They're adding up their dead and wounded to see how many they have before they come again, but there's still enough of them to finish us.'

'Did anyone see Estrada?' Frolech asked.

Drysdale was about to answer but then looked at Lindsay and cried in dismay, 'This *hombre*'s shot. He's hit bad.'

All eyes turned to Lindsay who had slumped into a sitting position against a rock. His shirt front was a mass of blood and even as the others watched he fell over on his side. The glazed look of his open eyes told the story.

'Ike!' There was a note of shocked disbelief in his voice as Frolech fell to his knees and turned his boss on his back.

'He's gone, Frolech,' Avery said without the slightest hint of sympathy.

'We'd better load our guns again because there's likely to be another attack.'

If Frolech heard, he did not show it. 'We was together right through the war. It ain't right that he should be killed by a lousy bandit.'

Locker said gently, 'We can't help him now, Herman. We have to get going.'

'Going?' Avery said in disbelief. 'Going where?'

'We have a chance to get away if we leave now,' the scout said. 'Those Mexicans have wounded men and horses and it will take them a while to figure who's fit to fight and how many healthy horses they have left. Chances are that Estrada was wounded — no one seems to have seen him — but these *hombres* probably know there's ten thousand dollars with us and a new leader could soon come to the fore if Estrada can't do the job.'

'There's nowhere to go,' Drysdale announced with a note of resignation in his voice. 'The Lipans are still out there somewhere.'

'Domingo said he'd leave a trail for us. It's our only chance.'

'I wouldn't trust him an inch,' Avery declared. 'He's probably a bandit too.'

'Hardly. When we were having our little discussion in Spanish he told me that he was the padre who posted the ransom letters.'

With a note of triumph in his voice Avery exclaimed, 'That's even less reason to trust him. He's on Estrada's side. You can't trust any of those psalm-singers.'

Locker was in no mood to argue. 'How would you know? You've probably never been inside a church in your life and have never seen the good work some of these padres do. He posted those letters in the hope of saving Dixon's life. If your stupid bigotry gets you killed, it serves you right. I intend to follow Domingo's trail whether you come with me or not.' He turned to the others. 'Anyone wants to come with me, come now because there's not much time. I'm going to tell Jenny if she hasn't already heard us arguing. She can take Lindsay's horse if she wants to come. What about you, Herman?'

'I don't like leavin' Ike here but I reckon that won't worry him now. I'll collect his guns and a few of his personal things and be with you in a minute.'

Locker hurried to where Jenny was holding the horses and wasted no time in advising her of the situation. 'If you want to come with us, come now. I reckon it's the only chance we have.'

'But I don't have a horse.'

'You have now. Ike Lindsay's dead. I'll shorten the stirrups on his saddle for you if you want to come with Herman and me.'

'What about the others?'

'They're still making up their minds. We can't afford to wait.'

'What about my money? I raised five thousand dollars for my father's ransom. Phil Avery has it. He reckoned it would be safer if he handed it over to the kidnappers.'

Locker had not considered the

money as being necessary for their survival but could see the girl's point of view. He told her, 'Get on that horse. If the stirrups aren't quite right, I'll try to fix them later. If Avery decides not to come with us, I'll get your money from him. Here's Herman coming now.'

The rifleman was carrying a bundle of his late friend's personal items — his gun-belt, and a calico money bag. After looping the gun-belt around his saddle horn, he began stuffing the rest into his saddle-bags and told Locker, 'I hate leavin' Ike to them human buzzards but there's no other way. What about the packhorse?'

'Leave it. Estrada's men might delay a bit longer sorting through the pack. I'm going now to get Jenny's money from Avery. Get mounted and be ready to ride. We are running out of time.'

Locker had no need to follow up his intentions because at that moment, Drysdale and Avery came running up.

'We're coming with you,' the detective announced as he took his horses' reins from Jenny's hand.

Drysdale also snatched his reins and almost threw himself into the saddle in his eagerness to leave the area.

Locker mounted and told the others to stay a few yards behind him while he tracked Domingo's mule. Secretly he feared that the padre might have made his tracks too hard to follow because if the tracking was too time-consuming their pursuers would soon overtake them.

Hoping that they wouldn't be observed, the party moved away through the sheltering brush. Frolech rode behind the others, glancing frequently over his shoulder and watching for the pursuit that he knew would soon follow.

Looking ahead, Locker saw a raw blaze on the trunk of a distant tree. Remembering Domingo's tomahawk, he realized that the conspicuous blaze was designed to save tracking time. He cantered up to the blaze and saw in a patch of soft ground where Domingo had turned to the south.

No longer worrying about tracks,

Locker led the party in the direction indicated, confident that when Domingo changed course he would leave a marker in some prominent place.

They had gained about half an hour when Frolech trotted up to the others and said, 'We'd best get movin'. I think I just heard a horse whinny behind us.'

13

It was not easy tracking Domingo's mule through the brush and Locker was worried that their slow progress was reducing their lead on the pursuit. He knew that their horses would leave a wider trail than a single mule and was also keenly aware of the quality of Mexican trackers. At what seemed a frighteningly slow speed they wound their way through a forest of cactus and mesquite. If the hunters caught them there, they could make no properly coordinated defence and their opponents could soon work around them undercover. One person might have been able to hide there but not a group of riders.

Then suddenly they were clear of the brush. A bare slope extended upwards for more than two hundred yards to what looked like a narrow pass on a high, steep ridge. The tracks of Domingo's mule showed plainly on the bare, red earth and they pointed straight at the pass.

Locker pointed to the notch in the skyline and called to the others, 'Get up there as quick as you can. Don't let them catch us in the open.'

'They'll see our tracks,' Avery said. 'Is there any way we can hide them?'

'Not a chance. Now, get going and stop just out of sight over the hill.'

Frolech steered his horse alongside Locker's bay. 'If we can get to the top of that hill, we can catch them fellas in the open. Gettin' across that open ground and up the hill could be mighty expensive for them.'

'That's exactly what I was thinking, Herman. We'd better get going so they don't catch us in the open. Let's try to find a good spot to spring a trap on them.'

With Avery leading, they galloped across the open, sandy flat and urged their horses up the slope. Much to everyone's relief, they gained the crest without incident and halted below it on the other side.

Locker dismounted, took his carbine and slung his box of quick-loading tubes over his shoulder. He passed his reins to Jenny. 'Hang onto my horse and wait here. Frolech and I intend to slow our friends down for a while.'

The rifleman also dismounted, handed his reins to Avery and followed the scout back to the top of the ridge. Taking up a prone position behind a clump of greasewood, he checked his rifle sights and whispered to his companion sprawled nearby under similar cover. 'How do you want to do this?'

'They're almost certain to have their best tracker riding in front. Could you hit him at this range?'

'I don't see why not. What are you plannin'?'

'I want them too scared to show themselves or get too close. Nothing slows down a tracker like the thought that he will be the first one shot. While we run, they'll chase us but if we turn on them a couple of times, they'll show us a lot more respect. If we damage them badly, they might decide that we're not worth the trouble.'

Frolech was more pessimistic. 'Those *hombres* know that we have ten thousand bucks between us. I reckon they'll see the risk as bein' worthwhile.'

They waited, studying the brush for the first signs of movement but their wait was not a long one. A string of hats suddenly appeared over the green foliage. Locker counted twelve and whispered, 'Here they come. Get the one in front. He'll be their best tracker.'

'We can get more of them if we let a few more come out into the open,' Frolech suggested.

'The others might rush us if we do. If they are close to cover, they're more likely to use it and we can gain time if they go to ground.'

A rider appeared at the edge of the ——sh. He checked his grey pony and ——— up at the ridge for a brief moment. The hoof prints of his quarry showed plainly on the bare red earth behind him. The watchers could not hear what he said but he twisted in his saddle to speak to another rider who joined him.

At that moment Frolech's rifle boomed and the foremost rider was smashed from his saddle.

Locker fired then at a second rider who was just emerging from the brush. This man too, went down. Too late, he saw the red shirt on the next horseman, who wheeled his buckskin pony about and disappeared into the trees. He was sure he was looking at Estrada even though the horse was different. He mentally reproached himself for firing too soon because they had lost their best chance to stop the pursuit.

Frolech had reloaded but could find no more targets and saw no point in wasting ammunition. He lay undercover, concealed and watchful.

'I think I missed a shot at Estrada,' Locker confessed. 'If I had looked at who was coming instead of taking the next in line, I might have got him. He's on a different horse. The other one must have been hit in our first fight.'

'Can't be helped,' the rifleman grunted as he surveyed the scene before him.

Gunfire started coming from the brush and puffs of powder smoke showed the rough location of the shooters but the men on the ridge did not take the bait. They knew they commanded the approaches to their position and were also aware that their enemies would soon test them to see if they were still in position.

By this time the sun was high and was beating down on the two men stretched out below. Both were thirsty, hungry and terribly tired but knew that they needed to lie quietly and wait.

The high crown of a Mexican hat showed briefly above a clump of bushes. It disappeared and then showed up again a few yards to the left of its original position.

'Don't fall for that old trick,' Frolech warned. 'They're just testin' to see if we're still here. That hat is probably on a stick. If we hold our fire, they might reckon we've gone and show themselves. We might even get another chance at Estrada.'

'What worries me, Herman, is that while we're waiting here, some of our chilli-eating friends might know a way of bypassing this place. It's still going to take time to pick up Domingo's trail again and I'm not sure how much time we have.'

The rifleman thought a while and finally suggested, 'Why don't you slide out and pick up the trail? I can hold things up here for a while. When you find where to go, come back for me and we can skedaddle in a hurry. You might even find a place where we can play this trick again.'

Locker agreed that the plan was a good one and crept away. He returned to the others, explained the situation and retrieved his horse. Picking up the tracks of Domingo's mule, he followed it into a labyrinth of brush-choked, heavily eroded, small canyons. He found a couple of broken branches in places where the tracks would be lost on rocky ground and then decided he had come far enough.

Frolech's rifle boomed again as he rejoined the others. A few scattered shots came in reply but then the roar of the .50/70 announced that the rifleman still controlled the approaches to the ridge.

'The way's clear ahead,' the scout announced. 'You'd best get mounted. I'll get Frolech and we can get out of here.'

'Time to go, Herman,' Locker whispered as he crept up to where Frolech was carefully studying the scene ahead of him. 'Did you get any more of them?'

'I got one with my last shot. I don't know how bad he was hit but sure as hell, he ain't laughin'.'

They crept away to their horses and mounted. Locker took the lead and they followed him along the trail he had scouted. The party would leave more tracks than Domingo's mule and they would be easy to follow but the fear of another ambush was firmly planted in the pursuers' minds and they would be more cautious, travelling slower, searching for trouble that was no longer there.

Avery was riding beside Locker and told him quietly, 'We'll have to find water soon. These horses have had none since yesterday and we don't have much left in the couple of canteens we brought with us. There's no grub either.'

'I know that and I feel I could sleep for a week but Domingo's headed somewhere and following him is our best hope.'

'More likely he's leading us into a trap. I don't trust him.'

Locker took the lead again as the country became rougher, and in places they had to push through masses of chaparral. The trail was getting harder to follow but occasionally he found deliberately broken bushes that told him the direction to go. Though he said nothing to the others, he too was having doubts. His sense of direction told him that their path twisted and turned more than seemed necessary.

They were moving in deep shade close to a canyon wall when he saw a streak of green moss on the rocks above. Then, when he rounded a boulder, there was a trickle of water flowing into a gutter of worn stone at the base of the cliff.

'There's water here,' he said quietly. 'Bring a couple of those canteens up here and fill them. Then bring the horses up one at a time.'

As they were filled, the canteens were passed down the line to the parched fugitives. The horses could smell the water and eagerly pushed forward. One after another the thirsty animals sucked up the refreshing water before being led away to make room for the next.

Greatly relieved Locker was about to continue the journey when the Mexicans stepped out of the brush.

14

Locker's first reaction was to start shooting and he had a gun halfway from its holster before he realized that the newcomers were not carrying any weapons. They were an old man, a middle-aged one, another slightly younger and a pair of teenage boys.

'Do not shoot,' a voice commanded and Domingo stepped into view, putting himself between both parties.

'What's going on, Domingo?' The scout's voice was heavy with suspicion.

'I am glad you followed my advice. I feared you would not.'

'Talk fast, Domingo. We're in a hurry.'

'I know the danger you are in and know we must act quickly. I want you to hand over your horses to my people. They will lead Estrada away, lose him and return your horses in a day or so, fed and rested.'

Avery heard the exchange and snarled, 'I'm not handing over my horse to any greasers. I don't know what game you're playing but I do know that this trail has been leading us south and we need to go north. Estrada's on our trail and we can't waste time arguing. Anyone coming with me had better come now. Anyone fool enough to believe this skunk deserves what he gets.' He glared around at the others. 'Who's coming?'

Drysdale urged his horse around the others. 'I'm with you, Avery. I know this country a bit and reckon I can get us back from here.'

'No one else? What about you, Miss Dixon?'

'I'll take my chances here. And one more thing — please hand over my money before you leave.'

'I don't see why I should. It will only go to these bandits if I do. I'll hold it for safe keeping and you can get it from Pinkertons if you ever get back.'

It was the ominous double click of

Locker's gun that resolved the issue. 'You're about three seconds away from getting a window in your skull, Avery. You know damn well that the money is not Pinkertons'. I won't let you steal it. Drop your saddle-bags and get riding. There's no time to waste and I'll kill you if you don't do as I say right now.'

The detective knew that Locker meant every word and decided that his life was worth more than money. Reluctantly he turned in his saddle, untied the strings and let the bags drop. 'It won't do you any good,' he muttered savagely. 'Come on, Drysdale. There's no time to waste talking to fools.'

The two riders spurred away into the brush.

When they were gone, Domingo spoke a few urgent words in Spanish and his helpers appropriated the horses. After a few more hurried instructions, they started out on the same course that Avery and Drysdale had taken.

The middle-aged man and one of the boys had been left behind and at

Domingo's orders they started out brushing away any signs of the meeting that had taken place.

'Follow me,' Domingo told the others. 'It is not far.'

There was no path to follow and Jenny was near exhaustion; her long skirt, catching on bushes, further hampered her progress and Locker spent a considerable amount of time untangling it. He knew that torn cloth or broken bushes could attract unwelcome attention in a land that, although it seemed empty, was well populated with enemies.

Frolech followed the other two with his rifle in the crook of his arm, Lindsay's saddle-bags slung over his shoulder and a suspicious look in his eye. He too had some reservations about their guide although he said nothing.

Finally they halted at a rocky overhang screened by bushes. Only when they passed through the foliage did they see that the rocky ceiling covered a large sheltered area. A circle of stones showed where a fire had once burned, although no smoke or spark now showed from the ashes. Blankets, a couple of boxes and a clay water jar were arranged against the back wall.

'Come in and make yourselves at home,' Domingo invited. 'It might not be very comfortable but it is as safe as anywhere around here. My friends have brought us some food. Cold tortillas and cold roast goat might not seem very appetizing but I dare not light a fire. Be seated and I will get out the food.'

Remembering how long it had been since they had eaten, Locker said, 'That grub sounds pretty good to me.'

Jenny found a flat rock, dropped the saddle-bags she was carrying and gratefully seated herself. Physically and emotionally she was almost at the end of her endurance but she was determined not to be a burden to the others.

No plates were available but the party had long since forgotten about such details. They held the food in their bare hands and attacked it with relish.

With the meal over, Jenny and Frolech stretched out on the ground and were soon asleep but Locker's curiosity had the better of him. He walked across to where Domingo sat keeping watch through the shrubbery. Always favouring the direct approach, he asked, 'What's going on here, Domingo? Why is a padre skulking around the country like a criminal?'

'Because, in terms of the constitution of 1858, I am a criminal.'

'How's that?'

'By law I cannot wear clerical garb outside a church, nor can I perform any religious functions outside a church. If, in the course of a sermon, I say something that can be considered as even mildly critical of the government, I am facing five years in prison. Weddings and funerals are now civil functions. A great number of churches have been seized by the government so that people in outlying areas are deprived of religious consolation. But many people still are faithful to the old ways and I must minister to their needs in secret.'

Locker looked doubtful. 'That's a bit different to what we have been told, Domingo. We are told that your church came back into power here when the French and Austrians laid claim to Mexico.'

The padre shook his head. 'I am afraid that your government would say anything that would help drive a European power from their borders. The Austrians were a little more tolerant and allowed the Church some concessions but the French held the real power and they were strongly anti-clerical. Maximillian's short reign did not relieve many of the previous injustices and when he was executed, it suited Juarez to claim that we were not loyal Mexicans and to renew our oppression.'

'What do the ordinary people think?'

'They might be poorly educated and have no voice in Mexico City but they are not fools. I still have many good friends. The people helping us today are some of my parishioners. They have shown me secret trails and places of refuge right through this area.

'My people will lead Estrada's men away with your horses. One rider splitting off the trail at a spot where tracking is difficult will not be noticed until suddenly the followers have nobody to follow. When your horses are fed and rested, they will be brought back one at a time by various paths.'

'What about the Indians?'

'It is safest to avoid them. I knew many of the older Indians because once, the Church acted as administrators on the Indian reservations, and some of these I can still count as friends. But in the guise of seizing 'Church' property, the Juarez government stole all the Indian lands, leaving them homeless. It is no wonder that the younger generation are hostile to Mexicans. Of necessity I must be wary of the Indians now.'

'How did you get mixed up with Dixon and Estrada?'

'Estrada grabbed me as an interpreter who could speak and read English. When

I first met Señor Dixon I saw that I had to devise some plan to free him from Estrada's grip. The ransom notes were the only way to save his life.'

'But why did you need two notes? Didn't Dixon trust our government?'

'Sadly, he did not. He told me that his death could be used by certain people in Congress seeking an excuse to start another war with Mexico. Also, if he arrived home and submitted a favourable report about the mineral deposits of northern Mexico, that could be an incentive for the seizure of more of our land. Some saw our struggling republic as a failure and were secretly advocating a United States stretching from the Canadian Border to Panama. To certain people he was more valuable as a dead martyr. Somehow he discovered that he was not working for a mining consortium but a group of very sinister people. That is why he suggested that we write another ransom letter to his daughter in case the first one was deliberately ignored.'

Locker shook his head slowly, almost as if rejecting what he was hearing. But now matters suddenly became clearer. 'I know now why everything was so secret. Ike Lindsay must have known what was going on.'

'He probably did,' Domingo said quietly, 'although he might have been deceived too. I do not know how Señor Dixon discovered the truth but he admitted being shocked when he found that the supposedly mundane task he had undertaken had such serious political implications. He might have been warned by a letter of some sort before he was kidnapped. I do not know. He told me that he had stopped his work and was making for home when Estrada caught him. There was much we could not say as his captors distrusted both of us and some of those present spoke a little English.' Indicating his battered face, the padre gave a rueful smile. 'I did not get my good looks kissing babies. Estrada's men have given me several beatings just to keep me honest, they say. Some government soldiers gave me the scar on my forehead as a demonstration of their patriotism. Your government might be praising Juarez for bringing liberty to Mexico but the commodity is only extended to those powerful enough to take it. My people are as downtrodden as ever.'

Locker was not particularly interested in Mexican politics and the views expressed, though disturbing, would have little bearing on the current situation. As he had different priorities, he changed the subject. 'How long do you think we will have to remain here?'

'I cannot tell. My people will return your horses when it is safe for you to leave. Estrada's men can be watched but the Apaches are totally unpredictable in their movements. It would not do to run into them accidentally. By avoiding Indian territory you must travel in more settled areas where Estrada would have spies. I cannot go with you all the way but will make a map for you. The trail will wind in unlikely places but it is safer than riding directly for the Rio Grande.'

'You can bet that's what Avery and Drysdale are doing. How do you rate their chances?'

Domingo paused and thought deeply before saying, 'As a man of faith, I cannot say that their position is hopeless but unless there is some form of divine intervention, their prospects for survival are not very hopeful. For all we know, they could already be dead at the hands of Estrada or dying by inches at the hands of the Apaches.'

15

Drysdale's desire to keep living had broken through his almost paralyzing fear and now he was using the variety of skills he had learned from years on the frontier. He had managed to conceal their tracks and already two different groups of horsemen had passed within earshot without discovering them. He knew they were Mexicans but was unsure if they served Estrada or were Domingo's men.

They had passed the night hidden deep in the brush. Drysdale's saddlebags had yielded a couple of strips of jerky and some hard ships' biscuit. The little water in his canteen scarcely allayed their thirst and finding more of the precious liquid posed a huge problem. Worse still, the horses had eaten nothing for more than a day and their flanks were hollow from thirst and hard usage.

'These horses might get us to the Sabinas River,' the scout said, 'but there ain't much more left in them. In a straight line they should just reach it although there's some mighty rough country in between.'

'Is there any other way north?' Avery had serious doubts about returning to that particular location.

'It could be the safest way for us to go. That Domingo *hombre* headed south and anyone follerin' him wouldn't expect us to go back over our own tracks. Now we'd better get goin' while the mornin' is still cool and these horses are still strong enough to make reasonable time.'

Two hours later they were kicking their weary mounts through tangles of mesquite and thickets of various types of cactus and skirting sharp-edged patches of dried black lava. In places the two men sometimes dismounted and led the weakened animals up a series of narrow ridges leading to the main range. Slowly though, they were making progress.

'We're nearly at the top,' Drysdale said. 'Best if we rest the horses here. Someone might see us on the skyline if we stop there.'

'You're worrying too much about those Indians,' the detective said impatiently. 'Who would be bothered coming out here? There's no game that we've seen and no reason for the Lipans to be here.'

The scout's angry response brought Drysdale back to stark reality. 'We're the game. Don't you see that? And the Apaches reckon that's a damn good reason to be here. Our only chance of gettin' out of this mess is to be real careful and see trouble before it sees us.'

They halted in the shade cast by a large boulder and looked back over the rugged landscape they had just crossed. Suddenly Avery pointed to a ridge running parallel to the one they had ascended. 'Look, there's something flashing over there.'

Drysdale's fears returned with a rush. 'Apaches,' he croaked. 'They're signallin'. Must be more of the devils around here somewhere. They're on to us.'

'Are you sure? From where they are they wouldn't have seen our tracks. We kept in the brush all we could — '

Drysdale interrupted. 'Ain't you got any sense? Who do you think them signals are for? There's Apaches around here already and them coyotes over there are lettin' 'em know they've seen us.'

'So do we run, hide or fight?'

The panic-stricken scout was already mounting his horse. 'You do what you like — I'm runnin'.'

Avery saw no further reason to debate the issue and threw himself into the saddle as his companion was already spurring his mount to the crest of the ridge. Without Drysdale he had no idea of his whereabouts and was sure that the Apaches would find him before he found safety.

His guide turned along the ridge top when he reached it, riding hard for the main range and hoping to be over it before the pursuers discovered them.

The detective was twenty yards behind when he saw Drysdale spin his mount on its hindquarters and gallop back towards him. Behind the fleeing man, four Apache warriors emerged from the brush and urged their ponies downhill in his wake.

A warrior fired in the air and in response to the signal, more riders appeared lower down the ridge, barring the path of the fleeing white men.

'Turn back!' Avery shouted. He had decided that two against four odds were better than being caught between two groups.

If Drysdale heard him, he took no notice and instead turned his mount down the steep side of the ridge. It was a risky move on a strong, fresh horse but doomed to failure on the exhausted animal the scout bestrode. It buckled at the knees, rolled sideways over its fallen rider and, in a cloud of dust, slid down the hill for a few more feet before coming to a halt against a tree trunk.

In his panic the fallen man tried to

get to his feet until a searing pain in his hip told the scout that something was seriously broken and that his run had ended. Death was staring him in the face and Drysdale preferred to go there on his own terms. He clawed at his holster and found that his revolver had been dislodged in the fall. He saw it in the dust two yards uphill from where he lay but for all the good it was it might as well have been on the moon. His carbine was likewise unreachable under his fallen horse, that seemed unable to regain its feet.

Avery chose the slim option of shooting his way out of trouble. Drawing his revolver, he fired at the oncoming warriors now only a couple of horse lengths from him. He did not know that his shot had missed because another brave had fired a charge of buckshot, a few pellets of which clipped his side and almost swept him from the saddle. Clinging to the horn with his bridle hand, he urged his mount straight at the nearest warrior. The jarring collision as the two horses met knocked the smaller Indian pony down. His own mount jumped awkwardly over the fallen animal and bolted madly up the ridge but in doing so, used up the last of its energy. Without warning, it grunted, staggered and fell. The detective was caught by surprise and the landing was hard but somehow, he retained the hold on his gun. Dazed with shock and half-blinded by dust, the Pinkerton man fired at the warrior, who was galloping towards him. The man threw up his arms and fell from his pony.

With the closest threats out of the fight, the detective ran to his horse which had struggled to its feet. He wasted no time trying to mount the exhausted animal but snatched the repeating carbine from its saddle scabbard. He fired a close-range revolver shot into the animal's brain and as it collapsed, dropped behind its carcase.

The few pursuing Apaches saw no prospect of overrunning their prey without serious losses and spun their mounts out of the fight, racing down each side of the ridge's bare spine and dismounting as soon as they were out of the line of fire. Then, firing the occasional shot to keep Avery occupied, they began to work around his position.

Not far away, Drysdale was ignoring the pain in his broken hip and struggling towards his fallen gun. In agonizing pain he might have progressed a couple of feet when he saw a familiar figure sliding down the steep slope to where he lay.

'Tomás,' he gasped. 'Help me get out of here.'

The young half-breed's white teeth showed in a smile that could never be mistaken for being friendly. 'Help you out? After all the trouble I took to get you here. I have wanted you dead since I was old enough to know that you and your scalp-hunting friends killed both my parents. I went to Eagle Pass to kill you but then found you were coming back to where you could answer for your crimes in a much better way.

Avery needed me and you thought I would be useful for any of the more unpleasant work. Things could not have ended better.'

'Tomás, you've gotta help me.'

'Drysdale, I want your knife. Where is it?'

The white man had forgotten his knife; it was under him on his belt. Painfully he twisted his body and reached for it, but Tomás was quicker. He caught the injured man by the shoulder, dragged him sideways as he screamed in pain and snatched the knife from his belt. 'Now you cannot kill yourself or anyone else. I know you won't be running away so I will leave you now until we kill Avery. Then we will be back to see you. I think we will enjoy your company more than you will enjoy ours.'

The young man disappeared over the crest of the ridge, leaving Drysdale vainly willing himself to die. But it seemed that while his mind was determined to die, his body was determined to live. He heard the shooting finally stop and the triumphant shouts of the warriors told him that Avery was dead.

Though incoherent with terror, Drysdale was still very much alive when, a few minutes later, a party of grim-faced Apaches came to where he lay.

16

For two days, Jenny, Locker and Frolech waited at Domingo's hideout. The padre absented himself for most of the day but always returned with a meagre supply of food, mysteriously obtained from unknown and unseen people.

At night, strange Mexicans visited the camp. None stayed long, just exchanged short messages in hushed tones before disappearing back into the brush.

'I wonder what's goin' on,' Frolech said quietly. 'I don't like all this secret stuff. I hope Domingo is as friendly as he pretends to be. We have ten thousand reasons to suspect that his intentions might not be as honourable as he says. Maybe he returned Jenny's money to give himself a chance at gettin' the whole lot.'

Locker had his doubts too but did not express them. Instead he told the rifleman, 'It could be that he has to keep his operations secret. If the government knew he was moving around doing things they didn't approve of, they might throw him into the jug. So far he has saved our skins but we still don't really know what's going on. It might pay to keep your guns handy just in case this padre turns out too good to be true.'

'I don't know what to make of him,' Jenny said. 'He's very serious and doesn't say much and he looks more like a bandit than a padre. I have tried to draw him out about what happened with my father but all he could tell me was that he became ill and died. He thought it might have been pneumonia but was not sure. He did say, though, that Estrada did not treat him too harshly apart from keeping him a prisoner.'

Locker was tempted to ask if Jenny knew about her father's secret mission but then reminded himself that it was none of his business. In the back of his mind he had the feeling that the less he knew, the safer he would be on the other side of the Rio Grande.

The morning of the third day was a cold one and a fog was limiting visibility to a few yards. The party had awoken early and were forcing down an unappetizing breakfast of corn bread and cold bacon. Domingo had forbidden any fires in case they attracted unwelcome visitors.

He had been some distance away, reading from what looked like some sort of battered prayer book, when suddenly the others saw him jump to his feet. At the same time he laid a finger to his lips to indicate silence. Then all heard horses coming through the brush. They were not making much noise and the fog concealed them, but the sounds indicated that there were more than one.

Locker and Frolech drew their guns and looked about for defensive positions but Domingo remained standing in the open.

Shapes appeared through the mist, vague forms of men and horses, as yet unrecognizable.

A faint whistle sounded and Domingo relaxed. Seconds later a party of riders leading saddled horses came into view.

'It's your horses,' Domingo announced. 'Today we must move but thanks be to God, we have a fog to shelter us. We need to be well away from here before the fog lifts.'

Hurried packing ensued although the fugitives really had little to pack. Locker helped Jenny with her horse and held it while she mounted. The animals were well fed and rested and the cool morning had made them lively.

Domingo spent a while in quiet conversation with the men who brought the horses and walked over to the others, his face grave.

'My friends have brought some bad news,' he told them. 'The two who left us the other day are dead. It was the Apaches. My friends found their remains yesterday. It appears that one died quickly but the other was tortured to death. I do not wish to go into any further details.'

'That's awful,' Jenny said.

Frolech was less sympathetic. 'Serves the danged jackasses right.'

The look on his face showed that Domingo plainly disagreed but there was no time to argue. 'We must hurry,' he told them. 'It is best to be out of here before the fog lifts because Estrada's men will still be about.'

'Where are we going?' Locker spoke in a low voice as he knew that sound seemed to travel further in fog.

'We will go down to the foothills and turn north. There are villages on the way but we will try to pass unseen around them. I will escort you to the Sabinas river crossing and leave you there.'

'You've stuck your neck out enough, Domingo,' Locker said. 'Get us over the Sabinas and I know a secret crossing north of Eagle Pass where we can get over the Rio Grande.'

The padre smiled. 'I think I know that crossing and so do many others. Apache raiders, bandits, smugglers and even honest Mexicans have often used it. Only you Anglos think it is secret.'

'So you think Estrada will have it guarded?'

'He might, but you could be lucky. While he thinks you are in these mountains, he might have all of his men searching here. My friends are coming behind and covering our tracks but their own tracks might help confuse the searchers. They will leave ample evidence that they are Mexicans.'

By the time the fog lifted, the party was travelling north through the foot-hills of the main ranges. The country was still rough and they travelled slowly. On two occasions they saw distant villages to the east but Domingo led them through barren country where no one would need to go. Consequently they saw no one else.

They halted briefly at a secluded patch of grassland and allowed their mounts to graze while they devoured a small meal of plain food that Domingo had produced. Then they started their journey again.

It was late in the afternoon when they arrived at the lower reaches of the Sabinas River. The stream was wider than where they had crossed it previously but Domingo knew a safe ford.

The shadows of the mountains were creeping across the land when their guide finally led them to a sheltered camp. To the surprise of everyone but Domingo, a sack containing corn bread and a quantity of unknown, cooked meat was hanging from the branches of a tree together with a small amount of cracked corn for their horses.

All were amazed at the efficiency of their benefactors but Domingo shrugged it off when they expressed their appreciation.

'I have used these trails many times and I have good friends who know where to find me. These are people who have little but who are always ready to share.'

Frolech growled. 'Let's hope it's only your friend who can find you.'

Locker sat beside Jenny as they

hungrily bit into food that at other times they would have found uninviting and monotonous. The girl had never complained but was visibly tired and the sorrow of her father's death showed in her downcast eyes and serious expression. The scout tried to think of something comforting or cheerful to say but did not want to add to her misery with a poor choice of words.

Finally he took a chance. 'I know you must be feeling pretty bad about your father. Is your mother still alive?'

The girl said miserably, 'She died years ago. There's no one left except some relatives back in Missouri and I never did see much of them. Pa was reasonably well off; he didn't need to be going around the outlandish places that he did but he was a restless man.'

'Let's hope he's resting now. Domingo would know more about that than I would but it would be nice if he was with your mother somewhere.'

Her smile was small and sad but at least it was a smile.

For another hour they sat and talked quietly, almost forgetting the danger still hovering around them like an unseen predator. Finally exhaustion took its toll and Jenny excused herself and sought her blankets.

Domingo roused them all while it was still dark. 'I must leave you,' he said. 'There is a wedding I must perform in a village not far from here. Señor Locker will know the way when it is light. I will pray that you get safely home.'

'We'll be sorry to see you go,' Frolech told him. 'Could we give you something for your trouble? You and your people have helped us a mighty lot.' Then he had a thought. 'Could you use Ike's Winchester and his six-shooter?'

'The rifle would be useful, señor. My people need to hunt a lot of game to keep their families fed but the revolver is just for shooting people and already there is too much of that.'

'There's some folks need shootin' too. Don't tell me you wouldn't kill a bad man to save your own or an innocent life.'

'I pray that such a situation will never arise for me.'

'I'm tellin' you now, my friend, that those situations can come up damn quick and when they do, you shoot first and worry about soul-searchin' later.'

Frolech brought over the rifle and a box of ammunition that had been in Lindsay's saddle-bag. He passed them to the padre who secured them among the untidy heap of belongings packed on the mule. For a second he held Lindsay's holstered gun in his hand and finally asked Jenny if she would carry it on her saddle. He explained that he was trying to lighten the load on his own mount and hers had the lightest rider.

Domingo finished his preparations and gave Jenny a handdrawn map that would guide her to her father's grave. Although exhumation was highly unlikely she would be comforted by the knowledge that Dixon had a known burial place. Then he solemnly shook hands with them all and gave another map to Locker with final instructions. 'Give me about half an hour before you leave the camp. That way you will not be caught if I should meet trouble. Have a safe journey, my friends. *Vaya con Dios.*'

Jenny spoke for them all when she said, 'Thank you, Domingo. We won't forget your kindness.'

He shrugged his shoulders and said dismissively, 'It was nothing. Many others would have done the same.'

'That's funny,' Herman remarked. 'I don't see them around.'

For the first time they heard Domingo laugh. 'I fear you have spent too much time with the wrong people, my friend. There are more good people about than you realize. Do not be so suspicious. You would be surprised how many total strangers have helped you get this far. They want no reward but help because they feel it is right to do so.'

Frolech remained unconvinced. 'That may be, Domingo, but I figure that Estrada would also feel it would be right to help himself to anything he could get his thievin' paws on.'

But Domingo said no more. He mounted his mule and halted a few yards before he disappeared into the still-dark brush. He raised his right hand in a blessing and rode into the gloom.

Frolech pushed back his hat and scratched his head. 'I still reckon there's somethin' funny about that sin buster. Why would he do all this stuff for us and get nothin' back out of it? Bein' naturally suspicious, I wouldn't be surprised if he was settin' us up for somethin'.'

Locker made no comment. He wanted to believe that Frolech was wrong but feared there might be some truth in the rifleman's assessment.

Jenny had no such doubts and leapt to the padre's defence. 'He's doing what he's supposed to do. He's helping people and taking big risks to do it. Don't you know a good person when you see one, Herman?'

'I ain't sure,' the other replied

seriously. 'Could be that I've spent too much time around bad ones.'

Locker reminded the others, 'You'll be spending a lot more time with bad ones if we don't stop talking and get moving.'

17

Locker watched the sun rise the width of two fingers above the eastern horizon. 'We've given Domingo his start. I reckon now it's time for us to go. We should reach the Rio Grande before dark tonight.'

'You might be a bit later,' Frolech said casually as he walked over to his horse.

The scout turned to find himself looking into the bore of Frolech's revolver. Any suspicion that it was a bad joke was quickly dismissed. Men like Frolech, when they felt a gun was necessary, would not hesitate to use it. 'Don't do anything foolish, Bill. Hear me out and keep your hands away from your guns. I'll shoot if you make me and that will sure complicate things for all of us.'

Jenny, in a shocked voice, said,' Herman what are you doing?'

'You might not understand, Miss Dixon, but just do as you're told and this will work out well for all of us. Now, very carefully, Bill, unbuckle that gun-belt and step away from it.'

Something about Frolech's determined expression told the scout that it was best to comply; he had seen Herman kill men as though human lives were of little consequence. Carefully, he stepped away from the fallen guns. 'What's all this about, Frolech?'

'It's about the five thousand bucks that Forbes Crossen gave Ike for the ransom. I'm takin' it. I figure it's owed to me for years of takin' risks and doin' dirty jobs for the likes of Crossen. Let's say I'm startin' my retirement.'

'You mean you're stealing that money?' Jenny sounded horrified.

Frolech smiled. 'I guess some would call it that. But don't worry. I don't want your money — you raised it honestly. But this cash was probably raised by double-dealing and graft by a bunch of respectable crooks who lack

185

the guts to be real bandits. I don't feel bad about takin' this because I am only stealin' from thieves.'

'You don't know that for sure,' Locker argued.

'You're wrong there. Ike and I have done a couple of jobs for Crossen. Not all were as respectable as this one. The problem is that you and Jenny are honest and if you get back over the border, you will have to tell Crossen what happened. This way the pair of you can swear on a stack of Bibles that I took the money at gunpoint.'

'You won't get away with this,' Locker told him. 'These are powerful people. They're sure to send someone after you.'

'Let 'em. Crossen will never know if I'm in the United States or Mexico. Chances are that Estrada or someone like him might get me before I get over the border but I'll take that risk. I might even decide to stay in Mexico.'

'They'll track you down. You know better than me that you're double-crossing some mighty dangerous people.'

'That's not your worry, Bill. When I leave you here, Herman Frolech ceases to exist. I'm sick of this German name anyway; maybe I'll get myself a fancy French moniker, next time around.'

Locker was not inclined to argue for he could see that Frolech was determined to carry out his plan. Even if he had desired to stop him, he knew that any gunplay would almost certainly attract those who were hunting them. His most important task, as he now saw it, was to get Jenny safely back across the border.

Keeping his gun on Locker the older man backed cautiously to his horse and mounted. 'Don't try to follow me,' he warned. Then his tone softened a little. 'Best of luck to the pair of you.'

Wheeling his horse, he galloped away.

'I'm so disappointed in Herman,' Jenny said as the sound of the retreating hoof beats became more distant. 'Do you really think he would have shot you if you'd tried to stop him?'

'Maybe not,' Locker replied, 'but there's a lot I don't know about that man and misjudging his intentions could have proven fatal. Men like that don't joke when they draw a gun.'

'Do you think he'll get out of Mexico?'

'I don't know, but I hope he does. Come on, let's get moving.'

They kept in the rough country checking travel directions by the sun and following Domingo's map. Because it was not drawn to scale it was difficult to assess the distances between the landmarks that the padre had drawn but when they came to the various places, they were, fortunately, recognizable.

Locker looked for Frolech's tracks for fear that he would unconsciously follow them into an ambush. He had seen the other's prowess with a rifle and did not want to invite a bullet by appearing to track him. He was much relieved when Frolech's track moved to the high ridges that lay west of their course.

It was mid-morning when they

sighted a small village to their north-east. The field glasses revealed a cluster of flat-roofed, adobe houses and a few makeshift corrals. People were certainly there although none were visible from Locker's vantage point that showed only the backs of houses. Their path lay west of the village but was intersected by a broad, open plain. Anyone moving across the bare expanse was sure to be seen. A detour closer to the foothills in the west offered sufficient cover but it meant covering an extra couple of miles. The shorter route was tempting but Locker knew that Estrada was unlikely to have left this area unguarded. He felt sure that men would be watching the plain.

He quietly told Jenny, 'We're taking the long way around here. If I were Estrada I'd have men out there in the brush watching for anyone careless or impatient enough to try crossing that big flat. We could lose a fair bit of time but it's best that we stay undercover and go around it.'

The girl agreed and they started

slowly picking their way through tangled brush, cactus and boulders. Periodically, Locker would stop and scrutinize the edges of the brush, looking for the men he suspected would be lurking there.

They were well into their journey before his caution paid off. It was the movement that first caught his eye. When he focused his glasses on a patch of trees some distance ahead, he caught a glimpse of part of a sorrel horse. Probably bothered by flies, the tethered animal was moving restlessly about. Eventually it moved enough for him to see that it was saddled but the cover was too good for him to see if there was a rider present. And if there were, he suspected that the man would not be alone.

Jenny was alarmed when he told her of his findings and even more so when he announced his intentions. She did not relish the idea of waiting with the horses while Locker scouted the position ahead.

'Be patient and wait for me here,' he

told her. 'It might take me a while to see what's happening with these *hombres* but I'll be careful and will come back for you.'

'See that you do.' She gave a nervous smile but days of hardship had given her an inner strength that Locker knew he could depend upon.

Fifteen cautious minutes later the scout had advanced to a place where he could see through a gap in the trees. Two horses were visible in the shade and he could see a man stretched out on the ground as though sleeping. It was siesta time but he doubted that both men would sleep at once. Where was the second man?

He edged closer, aware that he must discover the other guard before he was seen. A few more stealthy paces and suddenly he could see another pair of feet protruding from behind a boulder but there was something unnatural about their position. Puzzled, Locker halted and peered through the field glasses again. Closer now, he could see blood staining the shirt front of the man he thought was sleeping. Suddenly he understood the awkward arrangement of the legs he could see. He had seen it before on dead men. Restraining the urge to hurry forward in case the killer or killers were still in the vicinity, the scout continued his painstaking advance. Only when he was sure that no others were present, did he walk openly to where the dead man lay.

The ground was hard and showed no useful tracks but it was easy to see what had happened. The first man, a heavily armed bandit by all appearances, had been clubbed, probably with a rifle butt and a knife taken from the sheath on his belt. The second man had been fatally stabbed while he slept. The killer had then returned to his first victim and stabbed him to make sure that he never recovered consciousness.

The presence of the horses and the dead men's firearms ruled out the possibility of an Indian attack. Locker had no way of knowing whether the killer had been Frolech or even one of Domingo's henchmen but he knew he had to act quickly; a change of sentries could be due at any time. He ran back to where Jenny waited with the horses. He could see the look of alarm on her face as she watched him approaching.

'Bill . . . what's wrong?'

'There are two dead men with those horses, probably Estrada's men watching the plain for us. Someone killed them not long ago. We must take the short cut across the plain now. We need to be well away from here in case there's a change of sentries due. Get on your horse; we need to get across that open ground before someone else comes along.'

'Do you know who killed them?'

'I'm sure it wasn't Apaches. It might have been Frolech or even some villagers who don't like Estrada, but it has been lucky for us. Now let's ride while we have the chance and hope no one sees us.'

18

Estrada, with two of his men, found the dead sentries an hour after Jenny and Locker had ridden away. His surprise turned to fury as he saw how careless the sentinels had been. The loss of the men meant little to him but he was livid that the cordon he had thrown around the area had been breached.

'What happened?' he demanded of Diego, the squat, part-Apache tracker who always rode with him.

The little man glanced around. He could read the ground like a book. 'Two men have been here but they seem to have gone in different directions. Which should I follow?'

'Neither. These men were killed so that someone could get across the open plain without being seen by my men. Ride out on the plain and I am sure you will find the tracks of two riders. Call me when you do.'

The other man looked around the scene and, indicating the dead men, said, 'What do we do about these two?'

'Take their horses and weapons across to that village and tell the people there that my men will collect them later. We will leave those fools to the buzzards unless the people decide to bury them. I know that Padre Domingo is in this area somewhere. He might want to break the law and conduct funerals, but that's his problem. Now hurry because we will need to get after these two riders.'

Estrada waited until his man was well away and then started rifling through the pockets of his dead henchmen. The process gained him a few pesos and a gold ring, almost certainly stolen from one of the bandit's victims. Looking at the hills to the northwest he had a fair idea where the two riders he sought would be heading.

'You are not as smart as you think,' he said aloud. 'This is my country and even with the start you have, I know a few trails that will get me to the river before you.'

*   *   *

Once back in more sheltered surroundings, Jenny and Locker halted to give their horses a short rest. By standing on a boulder, the scout was able to get a partial view of the plain they had so recently crossed. He knew that plains are never quite as flat as they appear and that some low points could conceal riders but the lack of dust reassured him. On the thinly grassed plain, a large group of moving horses would make dust that he could see.

'Looks like Estrada hasn't found his dead men yet,' he said to Jenny as he climbed back down. 'I must admit, I was mighty worried there for a while.'

'How far are we from the Rio Grande?' she asked.

'A couple of hours' easy riding should see us there before dark.'

'What happens then?'

'My first job is to get you and your money somewhere safe. Eagle Pass is a mighty rough town and the country around is full of bandits, cattle-rustlers and dangerous types. It's no place for a lady on her own, 'specially when she's carrying a heap of money.'

Jenny patted her hip where she carried a small revolver under her serape. For the first time in their acquaintance, Locker heard her laugh. 'I'm a battle-hardened veteran now, Bill. I won't hesitate to shoot if I need to.'

'Let's hope that need never arises, but if it does, you're safer using Ike Lindsay's gun that's hanging from your saddle horn. Some of those little revolvers don't have much power; a determined man can often take a hit from one of those and keep coming. You might have to hold Ike's gun in both hands but it's the safest one to use.'

'I'll remember that. Now, what do we do when we finally get to Eagle Pass?'

Locker resisted the urge to tell her

that their safe arrival could not be guaranteed; there was no point in worrying her unduly. Instead he explained how he would have to send a telegram to Crossen advising of the situation and arranging the disposal of the horses and other equipment they had brought back. He would also assist Jenny in preparing a telegram to send to the Pinkerton Agency. Though she initially protested, the girl was happy that he would remain in Eagle Pass with her until matters were sorted out.

'What will you do when it's all over?' she asked.

'I have a bit of money put aside. I might head for northern Colorado and try my hand at ranching. What about you?'

'We own some property in St Louis but I don't want to stay there. I might sell up and buy somewhere further west. I'd like to buy a ranch and raise horses.'

'Much as I like horses,' Locker told her, 'the money is in cattle. Horses are cheap and you need to carry them too long before you sell them. The best compromise is to raise good cow ponies for your own use but rely on cattle to make the ranch pay.'

'Thanks for the advice, Bill. I'll keep it in mind. When all this is over and we have each gone our separate ways, it would be a pleasant surprise if our paths were to cross again sometime later as successful ranchers.'

'That would be nice, but right now we both have to follow the same path and it might still be a very rocky one. Let's get these horses moving again.'

'Do we have much further to go?'

'Not far now but we still need to be extra careful.'

★ ★ ★

Estrada and his two men had ridden hard. Horses were plentiful and cheap so there was no need to spare them. He knew that the people he sought would not attempt to leave Mexico via the official exit. Mexican Customs would surely find a pretence to confiscate all or part of the money they were carrying. They would head for the little-used and unguarded crossing some miles to the north-west.

The afternoon shadows were growing long when the trio spurred their failing horses into the shallow ravine that opened out into a large flat near the crossing.

'We will meet them here,' Estrada said. He pointed to the low ridge just south-west of them. 'They will come around the end of that ridge and will not see us until it is too late, because we will be in the shadow of the high ground to the west.'

He sent his tracker down to the crossing to ensure that their quarry had not somehow eluded them and smiled when the man confirmed that nobody had crossed recently.

With a clear view of the crossing and its approaches, the three men dismounted and waited. As he found a comfortable spot in the shade of a low tree, Estrada asked the man who had taken the dead men's horses to the village, 'Was Domingo at the village when you went there, Emilio?'

'Some claimed he was not and others said he had travelled straight through. He had certainly been there and maybe he was hiding. He sneaks around like a coyote preying on the superstitious ones. I don't know why the fools like him but they would not give him up.'

'He's harmless,' Diego said.

Estrada disagreed. 'Don't be too sure. He could be turning people against us. If they lose their fear of us, things might get very difficult. I think it might be time to get rid of that padre.'

'When should we do it?' Diego asked. He was not inclined to argue with his boss.

'There's no hurry. Sooner or later we will meet him on the trail and that will be the end of him. We can make it look like the work of Apaches in case someone asks questions.'

19

Though he said nothing to Jenny, Locker was growing anxious. All seemed to be going a little too smoothly. They were getting close to the river but there was a strange absence of tracks. He found it hard to imagine that Estrada would not guard the crossing if he knew of its existence and remained uncertain about the person who had killed the two sentries. It might have been Frolech but whoever it was did not seem to be heading for the river unless by another route. If another trail existed their enemies could get ahead of them without betraying their presence by horse tracks.

As they came closer to the river the country became less arid and a few larger trees grew among the mesquite and cactus. This meant that their approach to the river was more sheltered but made it more difficult to detect anyone who might be watching the crossing.

The river flowed sluggishly on their right, a wide expanse of brown water edged with reeds and trees. Across the water the steep, red bluffs of Texas looked invitingly close.

'We're nearly there,' Jenny said. 'Where do we cross the river?'

'Not far now. There's a trail down from the bluffs but it's hard to see until we get opposite it.'

'Domingo said there's a crossing here somewhere that a lot of people know about. Do you think that Estrada knows about it?'

'He ain't much of a bandit if he don't.'

This terse reply worried Jenny and she said anxiously, 'If Estrada knows about this place, won't he have it guarded?'

'He might unless Domingo's friends or even Herman attracted him in some other direction. If he reckons he's on a hot trail, he might call in all his men.'

Locker had been mentally rehearsing his answers to those questions for much of the afternoon. There was no point in worrying Jenny until he was sure there was a need. His hopes were rising as they approached to within half a mile of the crossing and saw nothing amiss. But previous experience with hostile Indians had taught him not to take situations at face value. He reined in the bay horse while they were still in a clump of mesquite and once more checked the scene ahead of them. On their right was a wide expanse of open ground leading to a sweeping bend of the river. The ground rose steeply on their left and while it might conceal dismounted shooters, there was no place to hide horses. The main danger lay directly in front where several erosion gullies ended at the river-bank. The ground was broken and boulders and patches of cedar provided ample cover for anyone lurking in ambush. Ominously too, the site commanded a good view of the crossing. A man with a carbine could easily hit someone at the water's edge or even out in midstream.

'Do you see anything wrong?' Jenny

asked. She was eager now to get back across the river.

'I can't see anything but let's wait another few minutes just in case someone gets a bit careless.'

'Do you really expect trouble at this stage?'

'If I were Estrada, I'd be watching here. Just because we can't see them it doesn't mean they ain't laying up in the brush over there.'

Locker's suspicion was more accurate than he realized.

Estrada and Emilio were resting with the horses in a dry channel carved by the floods. Diego was keeping watch, carefully hidden behind some low greasewood. He lay silent and unmoving except for his eyes that swept restlessly over the landscape before him. His hunter's instincts told him that the ones they sought would come soon and he was a patient man.

Locker located the crossing on the American side of the river. It was marked by a narrow, but clearly defined path up the bluffs. He pointed it out to

Jenny as a plan formed in his mind.

'See that path up the bluff? It looks steep but a horse can handle it easily. I think it's safest if you go first and if there is any trouble I'll cover you from here. We need to surprise anyone who might be waiting for us so I want you to ride as hard as you can. Don't stop for anything, no matter what happens. Keep going until you are safely up the other side. By the time you reach the American bank you'll be at very long range for a Winchester so keep moving fast and there won't be much chance of being hit. I'm hoping I am wrong and that Estrada is not here somewhere but we can't take the risk.'

'But what about you, Bill? I can't run out and leave you. Let's go together.'

'If something happens and I'm cut off, I can dodge around here. I know the country reasonably well so you have to go first and if any shooting starts, turn right on top of the bluffs and keep going until you reach Eagle Pass. I'll be along later.'

'But you'll be alone on the wrong side of the river,' Jenny objected.

'I can draw the fire away from you if any shooting starts and, if I shoot the right people, might even discourage any ideas of trying to stop me crossing. If there are too many I can lead them away. I know of other crossings I could use.' The latter statement was a lie but Locker knew it was imperative that Jenny should cross where she could. If things went wrong, he still had a very slim chance of eluding pursuit if alone.

Full of doubt, the girl studied the crossing until she was sure she knew the shortest way to reach it. Fixing her course in her mind, she gathered up her reins and jammed the big sombrero lower on her head. 'I don't like leaving you, Bill.'

'I'll soon catch up,' Locker told her with a confidence that he did not feel. 'Ride hard and don't stop till you are on top of the bluff.'

Dismounting, Locker levered a cartridge into his carbine, checked the sights and said, 'Go now.'

Diego was caught by surprise when the galloping horse suddenly burst into view. With a warning shout, he jumped to his feet and threw his rifle to his shoulder. His target was a fleeting one and the range was increasing with every stride of the horse. The first shot missed, but his second shot would be more carefully aimed. He knew exactly where the horse was headed, aimed a little higher to compensate for the range and waited for Jenny to gallop into his sights.

Locker saw the shooter jump to his feet and after one wild shot, was taking careful aim for his second. Sighting quickly at the stationary target, he squeezed the trigger. Even as his target dropped from view, he saw the man's rifle falling from his hands. With grim satisfaction he noted that the bandit was either dead or severely wounded.

Estrada and Emilio jumped to their feet at Diego's warning and were running to the edge of the gully when their sentry came tumbling down beside them. One glance was sufficient to show that he was out of the fight.

Locker knew where to aim, though he could see no targets. Then two heads appeared over the edge of the bank. These disappeared again as he raked the lip of the gully, sending spurts of dust into the air where the heavy bullets struck. They did no damage but managed to distract the other two from shooting at the girl.

Jenny's horse was well out into the river making a cloud of spray as it plunged through the stirrup-deep water. A good shot might have been able to bring horse or rider down, but Estrada and Emilio had other problems. Crouching low, they still had not assessed the number of guns ranged against them.

Knowing that every second was vital, Locker dropped the empty rifle, vaulted into the saddle and spurred hard for the crossing. Every yard his horse gained was precious in terms of rifle range.

When the shooting stopped Estrada

moved slightly to another spot and raised his head to look around. The pounding hoofs had already alerted him.

'Stop him!' he called frantically to Emilio who was still looking in shock at Diego's corpse.

Locker risked a glance and saw Jenny urging her horse up the steep bank but then his horse tripped in a hole. It went into a couple of long, lurching strides and almost recovered but then hit another patch of rough ground and cartwheeled. By sheer luck Locker was thrown far ahead of the horse so it did not crash on top of him. Even as he rolled along the ground a bullet struck the dirt beside his face.

The fall was forgotten because he now saw two men with rifles firing at him. The range was long for his six-shooters but he had to fire back in an attempt to spoil their aim. Lying flat, the slight downward slope of the river's edge gave him some cover but Locker knew that his opponents would eventually hit him.

He could see Estrada in his red shirt but the other Mexican was closer. The Colt .44 cartridges in his revolver were capable of travelling the distance if given the right elevation but that would involve a considerable amount of guesswork. Even a near miss might throw the rifleman off his aim. Taking careful aim, he sighted over the man's head and squeezed the trigger. To his surprise Emilio staggered, tried to straighten up, folded forward and fell to a sitting position on the ground. He clutched his middle, writhed about, then realized his danger and tried to struggle away. He managed to crawl a couple of yards but then he slumped forward and lay still.

The bandit leader was unsure whether Emilio had been wounded by great skill with a revolver or by sheer luck but he took no chances. Instead of advancing, he moved further back to where he could use his carbine to full advantage.

Locker's horse had climbed back to its feet and was standing nervously about fifty yards away tangled in the reins. However, there was little chance that he could get to it and ride safely away; man and horse would be easy targets for Estrada's Winchester. He tried another long shot.

The bandit's derisive laugh told him that he had missed by a fair margin. With one gun fully loaded, Locker punched the empty shells from the other and reloaded all chambers. One way or another he suspected that the battle would be ended by the time he had fired all twelve shots.

Estrada fired again and the bluffs on the other side of the river echoed back the sound of the shooting.

Locker rolled sideways narrowly escaping another bullet and though he fired back, it was only in an attempt to distract his opponent's aim. He jumped to his feet and sprinted a couple of yards, zig-zagging and trying to close the range. When next he went to earth it was at a lower point that offered only slightly better protection than his previous position.

Another Winchester bullet passed perilously close. Hoping that Estrada might have raised his rifle sights to give better command of the crossing, Locker sprang to his feet, advanced another couple of yards and threw himself sideways again. His only hope was to get into mid-range where a carbine sighted for two hundred yards would be shooting slightly high. The range would still be too great for accurate revolver shooting but his first priority was staying alive.

A couple of shots sounded behind him and Estrada's next bullet did not even come close. He had fired at something behind Locker.

A quick glance showed why the bandit had switched targets.

In a shower of spray, Jenny was racing her horse back across the river and firing as she came. None of her shots was likely to hit the mark but it diverted the Mexican's attention and gave Locker time to close the distance a little more.

Now Estrada centred all his attention on the approaching rider. Gambling that he was safe from pistol shots, he stood out in the open and sighted carefully on Jenny.

Locker fired as quickly as he could pull the trigger, anything to upset the rifleman's aim. The shots were echoing back from the bluffs and Jenny was firing too, even as she charged directly into Estrada's sights. The best that he could hope for was that the bullet would hit the horse and not the girl.

With one gun empty, Locker shouted as he drew his second Colt, trying to distract the rifleman. Sighting high, he was trying to judge the correct elevation for his shot when he saw his target spin and fall. It was hard to imagine that one of Jenny's wild shots had struck home but it was no time to be examining the situation. He ran straight at his fallen opponent.

Estrada was still alive and, with feeble movements, was trying to lift his fallen rifle. Then suddenly the effort seemed too much and he rolled back on the ground. But the will to live or the desire for vengeance drove him to grope blindly for the rifle again.

Locker stopped a few yards from him, sighted carefully, and shot him in the head. Estrada's body twitched once and then relaxed to sprawl unmoving, his blood soaking the ground.

Scarcely believing his good fortune, he turned as Jenny reined in her dripping horse. Anger at her disobedience and anxiety for her welfare were forgotten as he saw her pale-faced and shocked but still clutching her gun and grimly determined.

'Jenny, it's lucky you weren't killed. Why didn't you keep going like I told you?'

'We were in this together, Bill, and I don't run out on my friends. You looked like you needed help. Anyway, who died and left you boss?'

'Seems like Domingo must have been praying pretty hard for us. Who would have thought that you could hit Estrada with a pistol from that distance from a galloping horse?'

'I didn't shoot him. My gun was empty. You shot him first and knocked him down.'

Not bothering to conceal his surprise, Locker looked around and saw the body of Emilio, who had succumbed to his wound. 'If you didn't shoot him and I didn't shoot him, it only leaves that man over there but he was so far gone that I reckoned he was out of the fight. He's dead now and there's no gun in his hand. Why would he shoot his boss?'

Moving closer to Estrada's body Locker found a partial answer to the mystery. There was a bullet hole in the back of the red shirt. He looked at a brush-covered ridge directly behind where the bandits had waited. Nothing moved but he had the distinct feeling that they were being watched.

'Someone up on that hill shot Estrada. I don't know who did it or why and I'm not waiting around to find out. I'm going to catch that tangle-footed horse of mine and get back over the river before anything else happens.'

It was a greatly relieved pair of riders who splashed across the Rio Grande and set their mounts up the steep bank on the northern side. They halted at the top and allowed their horses time to recover from the steep climb. Using his field glasses, Locker studied the area they had left. He could plainly see the three dead men and then located their horses, still hidden.

'There's three horses down there in the brush. By rights I should have let them go but I didn't think of them at the time. I guess I'll have to leave them to whoever shot Estrada!'

'Who do you think it was?'

Locker looked back at the scene once more and put away the glasses. 'My first guess is that it was Herman. It would have been an easy shot for him and just because he was no longer with us, it didn't mean he was against us. We'd best get moving now because if it was him and he wants to cross the river I don't want to know about it. I might have to answer a lot of questions later and I want to be able to swear that I last saw him in Mexico.'

They mounted and soon picked up the trail to Eagle Pass. As they rode, Jenny said to Locker, 'It must have been Herman. He would have helped us out.'

'Whoever fired that shot might not have been interested in helping us. A man like Estrada has more enemies than friends and someone might have just taken the opportunity to have a shot at him while he wasn't looking. There would be a heap of people with old scores to settle — it might have even been a lone Apache interested in a bit of loot.'

'I still think it was Herman,' Jenny insisted.

'There's another likely suspect: what about Domingo? We know he was in the area and he had a good rifle and ammunition.'

'But he wouldn't kill anyone.'

'How do you know? If it meant

saving two innocent lives, he might shoot a known killer like Estrada. He could be able to shoot. There's a good chance that he might have to do a bit of hunting at times. We don't know a lot about him.'

'I know that he is a good, kind man and I would not like to think of him as being a killer.'

'As long as he kills the ones that need it,' Locker said, 'it won't greatly worry me. But the truth of the matter is that Estrada is dead and I don't give two hoots in hell who shot him before I did.'

'So what happens now?'

'Let's get back to Eagle Pass and take things one at a time. We both need food, sleep, and a general cleanup before we start worrying about anything else. I have a feeling that I'll have to do a lot of explaining before this mess is finished.'

20

Crossen was waiting in the same San Antonio hotel where Locker had first met him. The meeting had been arranged by telegram and the scout was uncertain as to how his employer would react to the news of the mission's failure and the loss of the money.

The big man wasted little time on pleasantries. 'So you're telling me that Dixon is dead?'

'That's right. I was told that he died of some sort of sickness, probably pneumonia.'

'Can you confirm this?'

'I was told by a Mexican padre who helped write the ransom note. He was a friend of Dixon. He buried him and gave me details of where he's buried just in case someone wants to dig him up later. I have no reason to doubt him.'

'And what happened to Lindsay?'

'He got killed fighting with the kidnappers. They had no intention of handing Dixon over; they tried to kill us and take the money.'

'What did Lindsay tell you about this job?'

'The same as you did. We were going to do a ransom deal. He didn't tell me anything about who arranged the deal or why it should be so important to certain people. Ike was pretty close-mouthed. He told me as little as possible and I have the feeling that the less I know about this deal, the better.'

'What about Frolech?'

Locker said in all honesty, 'That was a complete surprise. I never figured he'd pull a gun on us and run with the money. He struck me as a pretty dependable fella until he did that.'

'Would you be interested in going back to Mexico and tracking down that man?'

'There's no way I'll go back there. Personally, I think that there are mighty long odds against Frolech ever living to enjoy his ill-gotten gains. That area's crawling with bandits and stirred-up Lipan Apaches. Any group smaller than a troop of cavalry would be at risk down there. There weren't enough of us and I'm surprised that Frolech and myself weren't killed along with Ike Lindsay.'

Crossen's eyes narrowed and he leaned forward. 'You and Frolech weren't in cahoots were you, Locker?'

'Damn right we weren't. You can think that because I reckon you trust no one, but don't say it around the place if you know what's good for you. I have nothing to hide and did the job I was paid for. You recruited Frolech, not me. When I walk out of this building that's the last you and I will see of each other. This whole business is over. Let it die.'

'You will tell nobody about this.' The statement carried an implied threat.

'Don't try to frighten me, Crossen. Leave me alone and you have no worries but if you start bothering me, I know just enough to start digging and who knows, I might find out about the sort of game you're playing.'

'I had to ask those questions,' Crossen said. 'If you keep your word, I'll keep mine. Is there anything else?'

'There are two horses and saddles at Holloway's livery stable that belong to you. They're booked in under your name. Holloway will sell them for you if you don't want them.'

'Two horses?' Crossen looked suspiciously at Locker. 'Who rode the other one?'

'The other one was Lindsay's. Frolech wasn't interested in stealing it and I figured I might need another horse before I got this side of the Rio Grande.'

'I'll have someone attend to that matter.' The big man reached into an inside pocket and produced an envelope that he passed to Locker. 'Here's the balance of what is owed you. All things considered, you did as good a job as anyone could under the circumstances. Are you sure you wouldn't be interested in the odd job at some future time?'

'Thanks all the same but I intend

trying ranching. Better luck with your next job.'

Crossen turned and looked out the window. 'Thank you, Mr Locker. I doubt that our paths will cross again.'

Jenny was waiting at the hotel where they had each taken a room. The stylishly dressed young lady scarcely resembled the bedraggled figure who had booked into the establishment. She greeted Locker eagerly. 'How did things go?'

'Not too badly. I got the feeling that Crossen was relieved by the way things turned out. He wasn't impressed by Frolech's venture into private enterprise and offered me the job of going after him but I told him I wasn't interested.'

'Did he know about my part in things?'

Locker smiled as he said, 'I didn't want to worry him with matters that didn't concern him.' Then he asked, 'How did Pinkertons take the news about Avery and Drysdale?'

'They had been paid for their services in advance and didn't seem unduly upset about losing a couple of men. I had the distinct impression that they were no longer interested. It looks as though it's all over now.'

'There's one more job,' Locker said. 'I have to escort a certain young lady safely back to her home in St Louis. Then I might go looking for a ranch.'

Jenny smiled. 'I am only going home to sell up and then I'll be after a ranch myself.'

Locker's hopes soared. Their shared experiences had left him with another ambition that had nothing to do with business. 'What do you think of the idea of a partnership?'

She linked an arm in his and gave a smile that set his heart racing. 'I thought you'd never ask.'

THE END